RED-HOT REUNION

Trina wrapped her arms around Reno's neck, her cheek on top of his head. She pressed kisses on his head, eyes, and lips.

"Unwrap me," she urged.

"What?"

"I'm your make up gift." She stepped back just enough to pull at her belt.

"Trina, what are you doing?"

"Seducing you," she said.

Reno remembered every time he'd played the lottery. He could still recall every traffic ticket he'd almost beaten and every contest he didn't win. But with Trina he'd hit the jackpot . . . he just wasn't sure if the prize was going to cost him too much.

SUDDENLY SINGLE

CARMEN GREEN

Dafina
Books

Kensington Publishing Corp.

http://www.kensingtonbooks.com

DAFINA BOOKS are published by

Kensington Publishing Corp.
850 Third Avenue
New York, NY 10022

All Kensington Titles, Imprints, and Distributed Lines are available at special quantity discounts for bulk purchases for sales promotions, premiums, fund-raising, and educational or institutional use. Special book excerpts or customized printings can also be created to fit specific needs. For details, write or phone the office of the Kensington special sales manager: Kensington Publishing Corp., 850 Third Avenue, New York, NY 10022, attn: Special Sales Department, Phone: 1-800-221-2647.

Dafina and the Dafina logo Reg. U.S. Pat. & TM Off.

ISBN-13: 978-0-7582-1298-6
ISBN-10: 0-7582-1298-4

First mass market printing: March 2008

10 9 8 7 6 5 4 3 2 1

Printed in the United States of America

Chapter 1

"Trina, when we get married we can build an empire. With the strength of our combined families, we can take over the construction industry in the South. We could be the most powerful black family in the nation."

From her courtside seat at Philips Arena, Trina Crawford eyed her boyfriend Drake Plunkett and decided he'd had enough beer for one night. She casually moved his cup to the other side of her foot and turned her attention back to the Hawks dance team, who were shaking it up center court.

The arena was full even though it was Valentine's Day, and red and white ruled the crowd. A group in the yellow section tried to get the wave going and a smattering of people joined them, petering out halfway around the building.

"Why won't you answer me?" Drake's face pressed into her peripheral vision.

"I'm not interested in empires, Drake. My family has their businesses and I have mine. Suddenly singleatl.com is what I care about. Not combining anything for an empire, if I can be honest here. I don't want to get married, you know that. It's just not for me. I've told you that before. So, can we please drop it?"

He didn't answer so Trina pushed to find something else to talk about. "Do you want a hot dog?"

"Trina, I would appreciate you taking me seriously."

"I refuse to argue about this, Drake. So, no."

His brows bunched together over his rimless glasses. "No?" he repeated.

"I won't take this seriously because you won't take my desire not to marry seriously. We're at the beginning of halftime of the Hawks versus the Lakers. The only thing I'm concerned about now is the Hawks winning. Come on, D. Let's just lighten up."

"You know I hate when you shorten my name."

"I'm sorry." Trina knew that was one of his pet peeves, but why was it necessary to decide happily-ever-after here?

His presence had been suffocating lately, and Trina had been considering stepping back from their relationship now that she was about to devote a great deal of time to her new dotcom venture. But when she looked into his earnest eyes, she thought maybe she should cut him a break.

That's why she'd invited him to the game tonight. So they could have some fun without thinking or talking about anything serious.

"We're here to have fun. Come on, now." Trina tried to be playful with him and failed, so she left him alone.

Drake nodded his head and pulled out his BlackBerry. He tapped for a minute, then showed her the picture. She recognized the blueprint, but didn't know why he was showing it to her. "What's this about?" she finally asked, anger taking root in her stomach.

"This is my blueprint of a mixed-use community I want Plunkett/Crawford Enterprises to build in South Atlanta. The land had been vacant for years because of a court battle between family members, but that ended Friday. The final holdout died." His grin was smug. "I swooped in and picked it up for a song. Baby—" Drake smiled at his reflection in the BlackBerry and smoothed his perfect mustache down. "Plunkett Towers will one day be the Trump Towers of the South."

"Someone died and you got a sale? How's that possible? You took advantage of the family while they were vulnerable?"

His laugh told her she'd better recognize. "Look, sweetheart," he said, his voice full of condescension, "I took advantage of an opportunity. Believe me when I tell you that Westfall and Sons would have been at the hospital bed waiting for Henry Stone to take his last breath, had they known where he was. I *ran* into his daughter and connected them with a great hospice. It was the least I could do. He was there a day before he bit it. Naturally, the family chose me."

Drake looked like he wanted to stand up and take a bow. He settled for laughing and then checked the reflection of his teeth in his Black-Berry.

Seeing the shell of a kernel of popcorn, he

started digging with his fingernail, looking crazy as his whole hand nearly fit into his mouth.

Wincing, every couple jabs, he kept digging. Trina turned away. Drake was making a spectacle of himself.

He was ambitious and Trina understood drive and determination. He touted her family's attributes often.

Her grandfather and father were judges; her mother a black-belt martial arts instructor and mother of six. Uncles and aunts and grandparents were professors, doctors, dentists, world-renowned singers, bounty hunters, Marine Corps colonels. The list went on and on.

But they weren't bottom feeders.

Trina looked at the man she'd been dating for two years and wasn't sure she knew him at all.

Drake had always measured his success against Westfall, the biggest builder in Georgia. There wasn't a day that went by where he didn't show her an article or make a comment about how much property bore the Thomas Westfall name. He wanted to build an empire and she was just the adapter cord to the biggest plug in Georgia, her brother and cousins' Crawford Construction Company.

"Back to my main point," Drake said. "We will be one of the most powerful couples in the state."

Irritated, Trina looked at him. "You should have let them grieve in peace."

"They'll grieve better rich than poor." He leaned down so their arms touched. "If my architectural firm and Crawford Construction merge, we'll have a lock on the urban renewal projects and grants given to minority companies for those jobs."

Trina tipped her head, feeling her patience slipping along with her good mood. She and Drake never talked politics, but his Black Republican mentality was about to cause a fight. They'd agreed long ago to disagree on political parties, but Drake was trying to foist his lack of respect and disgusting greed upon her.

"I thought you didn't believe in Affirmative Action," she said, baiting him.

"I don't. Every man has a fair shot at any opportunity. However, in this instance one of the criteria is that I must be a minority to be able to bid on the jobs. This is called using your assets to your advantage."

His sharp bark of laughter and double foot stomp showed that he couldn't believe his good fortune. He was 'getting over.' "I'm so taking that money."

Shaking her head, Trina couldn't dislodge his hypocrisy.

"Why not bid on them the regular way? There's no reason to take something you don't believe in."

"Why go the hard way when it's not necessary? Taking the money is the American way. Anyway, let's talk about us. It's time for us to get married. Say yes."

Trina stared at Drake and wondered if he was intentionally trying to ruin her evening? Where had he been? Though sitting right next to her, he acted as if she hadn't said a word.

He knew the answer was no, *hell no* now, so why was he pressing the matter? And why was he now so intense? Was he trying to make a mid-night deadline?

Being at the Hawks game, full house of fans, the excitement high, this was supposed to be a fun night out, but Drake had to turn it into something that would end with one of them, *him,* being unhappy.

She touched his arm, peering into his deep brown eyes. Where had the easy-going man that she'd met two years ago gone?

The old Drake knew she never wanted to get married.

"Trina," Drake commanded. "Answer me."

"You didn't ask a question." Trina strained to keep her famous Crawford temper in check, but Drake was rounding third on getting told off. "Do you want more nachos," she asked him.

Drake slid to one knee, and his lips strained to grin around his professionally whitened teeth. If this had been an ordinary day with them sur-rounded by her family members, she'd have put him in his place, but this wasn't an ordinary day. Drake wasn't family like that, and she wasn't tempted to upgrade his status.

Trina stared at the only imperfection in this chino-wearing, pink-shirted, perfectly pressed boyfriend of hers.

He was never late. He wasn't mean. He knew how to manage money and he was passable in bed. He was the perfect black Ken doll.

Drake's problem was that his ideal life was one unending picture of the day before. In the two years they'd been together the only thing that had changed was his drive to conquer the real estate world in the South.

She couldn't help herself and looked away, wishing Drake would get off the ground and sit down. Halftime was almost over, and in a minute the Hawks were going to take the floor and show the Lakers who was boss.

"Drake, change the subject."

"Why?" Disappointment made him sound whiny. Trina braced herself for the aftershock of chills that always raced over her skin when his voice got just a little too effeminate.

She decided to pretend he was sitting beside her instead of kneeling. "Honey, after the game let's go dancing. My brother's band is playing. You know how much you enjoy hanging with them."

When he didn't answer she looked toward the tunnel again, and Drake moved to block her view.

Annoyed, Trina crossed her legs and looked Drake in the eye. "You know how I feel about marriage. I told you I didn't want to," she said more forcefully, "and you agreed. Right?"

Drake nodded.

Trina grabbed her purse. "I'm going to the concession stand. Do you want anything?"

The noise around them increased until Trina could hardly hear him.

"Don't be angry," he said, as cameras closed in like roaches at a preschool birthday party.

"Have we made a life-long love connection?" A familiar voice boomed, and Trina stared up at TV and radio announcer, Tippy Hudson.

The ageless broadcaster had been covering entertainment news in Atlanta since Trina was able to press the TV remote. There had been a young reporter sitting in to cover the entertainment updates on WSBM-TV of late, but Tippy was back. His skin was bronzed, his teeth capped, and way too white, and he sported a row of hair implants that were spaced just enough apart to look like he'd gotten the short end of a buy-one–get-one free deal. But his eye-lift said he was bushytailed and this was his coming-out party.

Trina now understood why there was so much press present. It was Valentine's Day, and tonight a lot of people's dreams were going to come true. Unfortunately, at least one heart would be broken.

"Tippy, do you mind," Trina said, "This is a private matter."

Trina tried to be as discreet as possible in front of nearly forty thousand people, but Tippy had the microphone pressed against her bottom lip.

"Are you Drake Plunkett and Trina Crawford?"

Tippy tried unsuccessfully to corral them into the center of the court. When he noticed that Trina wasn't following, he pranced back, turned sideways, and shoved the microphone between them.

"I know you're probably nervous," Tippy said, his smile encouraging her to say cheese for the cameras. "So why don't you tell us a little about yourselves. What do you do, Drake?"

"I own an engineering and architectural firm in Atlanta."

"And you, Trina?"

Pissed that she'd been set up, Trina put a smile on her face and, to Tippy's surprise, took the microphone and walked to center court with it.

"I'm Trina Crawford and I just started my own company, Suddenlysingleatl.com. It's a dating service that matches singles exclusively in Atlanta. So if you're single and free to date, you're welcome to join Suddenlysingleatl.com. Thank you. Goodnight."

Tippy gave her the evil eye as he wrestled the microphone from her hand. "Well, that was quite a free plug."

"Speaking of. You look really nice, Tippy. Really . . . nice."

Most of the audience chuckled, but Tippy wouldn't be dissuaded.

"Tonight is Valentine's Day, and it's a day for lovers. I believe Drake would like to end your single and free days. Drake!"

Trina crossed her arms and faced her boyfriend. How dare he force this on her? "Don't do this," she urged, anger shaking her voice. This was the part of marriage she hated. The sucker punch.

"This will be a marriage of purpose. We'll have a strong alliance, and the Crawfords and Plunketts will build empires. You'll see," Drake promised.

"This is your night," Tippy said, practically skipping. "Drake, are you ready to ask this lady the most important question of your lives?"

The audience was standing, many of the women with their hands covering their mouths. "Drake, stop now," Trina whispered through clenched teeth, trying to pull him away from Tippy.

Drake shook off her hand as he descended to one knee for the second time that night. He didn't *want* to hear her. He thought that if he did this in front of thousands of people she *couldn't*, no, *wouldn't* say *no*. She wouldn't embarrass him and she wouldn't embarrass herself. She was a Crawford and Crawfords had made a name by helping people and always keeping things positive.

Trina's relationship with Drake flashed through her mind like a thousand single frame snapshots.

Drake thought he knew all about her because he'd been hanging around her family for two years under the auspices of being her boyfriend.

But he'd really been studying her family. Sizing them up so that he could see *his* dreams come true. She was the catalyst to his thirty-year plan.

He'd said nothing about love or wanting her or even needing her. Just about an alliance between the families. She'd been a test, but he'd missed the most important lesson of all. He didn't really know the woman he wanted to marry, and tonight was his final exam.

The roar of the crowd filled her ears.

"Trina." Drake's voice boomed throughout the arena. He looked up at her, and his eyes reflected smug confidence. "Will you marry me?"

She waited for complete silence, leaned in and said firmly, "No."

Her voice hit every corner and flashed on every scoreboard.

The crowd reacted with boos and cheers, and Tippy looked like he was going to wet his pants.

Walking back to her seat, Trina started clapping. The Hawks were taking the floor, and she'd just become suddenly single.

Chapter 2

Reno Merriwether searched for a comfortable position in his leather recliner, chips and beer perched on his thighs.

He tried to relax, but he hated this chair. He hated the flat tan color, and he hated the inexpensive leather sticking to his skin.

Divorce had squeezed his budget super tight, but as soon as the contracts were finalized for the deals he'd made last month, his recycling company would be well in the black, and he'd be able to buy anything that he wanted.

He sipped his beer, focusing on the TV screen when he realized that a commercial was playing. Hitting the forward button for the TiVo, he flipped through the advertisements.

The phone rang and he warred with picking it up, then grabbed it before the fifth ring.

"Merriwether here."

"Mr. Merriwether, this is Mrs. Elmi from the Mandela Adoption Agency. May I have a word?"

"Certainly. What can I do for you?"

"We received your paperwork and it's complete except the section about your wife."

"Yes, Mrs. Elmi. I was going to call about that. Will that be a problem?"

"If you are not married? Yes, indeed. You see, the agency only allows married couples to adopt the children. Or the adoption cannot take place. How is Chloe?"

"She's fine. Beautiful." Physically she was as perfect as any child could be. But with the events of the past year, he couldn't say she was well-adjusted mentally. She hadn't said a word in ten months.

"That's so good to hear," Mrs. Elmi said. "Some children have adjustment issues, but if Chloe is doing well, then it will be even better when you have the sisters together."

"Yes, it will. We're excited about Christina becoming a member of our family."

"Are you married, Mr. Merriwether?"

Reno considered lying, but couldn't. "No. My wife and I divorced a while ago. But I will be married by the time we get to Africa. Does Christina need anything?"

"Unfortunately, we cannot take anything specifically for her, but the children could use socks and baby wipes, toothbrushes and toothpaste. But adopting Christina into a good home is our greatest prayer."

"Yes, ma'am." He did the mental calculations and figured if he spent a few hundred dollars on the items she mentioned, the kids would be set for at least a year. "Mrs. Elmi, we'll be there in six weeks."

"Please bring all the necessary documentation of your marriage and Chloe's final adoption papers. Good evening, Mr. Merriwether."

"I'll send a box of goodies this week. Goodbye."

Reno sat through another round of commercials, processing what he'd just said and wondered what he'd tell them when he arrived with no wife. Surely a happy home mattered more than the sum of its parts?

The last sip of beer slid down his throat and he went to the kitchen for another and sat through a commercial about the new Dodge truck when he caught himself.

His concentration was shot.

His life had been very different just three hundred sixty-five days ago. His job had been hectic, but he'd been married and his daughter had talked.

Ever since her mother left nine months ago, Chloe had said fewer and fewer words until one day she'd stopped talking altogether.

The lights in the den flickered off and he glanced over at the most important person in his life. She wasn't more than two-and-a-half feet tall, but love for her filled all his empty places.

"Hey, baby. Can't sleep?" *Please talk to Daddy.* As the psychologist had warned, he didn't push. Chloe would talk in her own time.

Her little head rocked from side to side.

It was bedtime. She should have been asleep an hour ago. His ex-wife Dana had told him repeatedly to keep to the schedule they'd established since adopting Chloe.

But nothing was the same. His baby didn't talk. And Dana was no longer with them.

He patted his thigh and Chloe scrambled up with June, the bear, under her arm.

Reno handed her a chip, another no-no, and they settled back. He tickled her neck and she squirmed, but no little girl giggles gushed from her the way they used to. She didn't even call his five o'clock shadow Freddy because it scratched her cheek.

Chloe said nothing.

Soon she turned sideways and began to bump his chest with her shoulder, which meant she wanted him to rock her. At least she'd come to him this time instead of tearing up her bed. He rocked her, watching commercials because Chloe liked them.

The game came back on.

"This Hawks vs. Lakers game will be remembered not because of what happened on the court between players, but what happened on the court between couples celebrating Valentine's Day moments ago," Tippy Hudson cheerfully recounted, with his big white teeth. He looked like an overdone bad wolf from the fairytale. "Let's show the clip."

Reno aimed the remote, then lowered it when the familiar face appeared. He sat forward shocked.

He remembered Trina Crawford well.

She was still a gorgeous woman, with womanly

curves, and her hair in natural curls cascading around her face and neck. Gone were the glasses, braces, and the long hair of freshman year, leaving behind a beautiful mature woman.

Reno barely heard her boyfriend speak, except to note that his voice was annoying. He focused on Trina who spoke of her company, and he logged the address in his memory to check out later.

Reno leaned back, glad she was doing well.

She'd always been ambitious, but the Crawfords were a successful family that bred talent from the womb. From the time he'd met Trina as a freshman on the basketball court his sophomore year, he'd known she was special.

She'd been the first girl to slam dunk in the college gym. She'd done it the first game of the season and ten games later she'd amazed the crowd and done it again.

Trina had made history, and had been his first love.

Now she was glaring at the man in front of her, her hands on her hips. The man was on bent knee, a ring box in his hand, and he wasn't tapped in to the obvious.

Dude, she's about to blow.

Reno grinned despite himself. This was gonna be good.

"Will you marry me?"

Although Reno knew what was going to come out of Trina's mouth, he still held his breath.

"No!"

Her answer was as quick as her jump shot had been.

Reno swore, then bit his tongue. He expected to see Chloe's little mouth curled into an *O*, but her head rested against his chest. She'd fallen asleep.

He let out a relieved breath, his attention on the TV drama.

Trina didn't acknowledge the man or Tippy, who looked like he'd just been kicked in the nuts. She walked off the court back to her seat and was clapping when the Hawks took the court.

"She's staying for the game." Reno stomped his foot, laughing. Trina still had bigger balls than most men. He cheered her bravado.

The sad truth was the way the news recapped Trina and her boyfriend's evening, and the world could see that she'd said no at least once when they'd been on the sidelines. The guy hadn't listened and had pressed her.

TV cameras and photographers were gathered around Trina to get the best shot of the woman who'd turned down a marriage proposal *and* stayed for the game.

"Who is she?" the sports announcer asked Tippy. "Steroids be damned. I want some of the protein she takes for breakfast."

"I don't know if it's protein or good genes. Trina Crawford is the daughter of Atlanta attorney Julian Crawford. Her grandfather is the Honorable Judge Julian Crawford, Sr., her grandmother, Vivian, was a professor at Spelman College. Her family members are quite established in the Atlanta community.

"Trina was somewhat famous in her own right as an athlete. Back in her University of Georgia days, she was the first woman to slam dunk."

The announcer looked suitably impressed. "Tippy, you never cease to amaze me. Well, Ms. Trina Crawford is no shrinking violet. I'm sure we can expect more of the same now that she's entered the dotcom world with Suddenlysingleatl.com. Best wishes to Trina Crawford and Mr. Plunkett," he added with a chuckle. "Back to the game between the Hawks and the Lakers."

Reno got up and tucked his daughter and June back into bed. He sat with her for a few minutes watching her breathe, making sure she didn't awaken and become frightened when she discovered she wasn't with him. After he was sure she was okay, he kissed her downy soft hair.

Months ago he'd stopped tearing up after she'd fallen asleep. His heart was heavy as he gazed at her from the door. As a precaution, he checked the baby monitor to make sure the battery light glowed green, then closed the door and returned to the den.

As he sat, memories rushed back like hot lava as their last physical encounter bubbled up from the archives of his mind. Seeing Trina again brought back the remembrance of every caress of her fingers on his cheeks and arms, every lick of her tongue over the warm skin on his back, and the way her misty gray eyes implored him to stay with her as they sailed seconds apart into paradise.

He remembered making love to her had been the single most important event in his life until he'd fallen in love with the woman who'd become his wife and now his ex.

Reno quickly reversed TiVo and stopped at the photo of Trina cheering the Hawks onto the court. She was smiling as if she didn't have a care in the world.

Reno knew that wasn't true. He'd known her to be an emotional young woman, affected by politics, society, and women's issues, but mostly by family. Trina had been one of many kids and hadn't always liked it. She'd wanted to be known for her own individuality. She'd always wanted her own business. Now she'd done it. Suddenlysingleatl.com. That was so Trina.

Her smile captivated him. He remembered her full lips, her sexy feet that went from sneakers to sandals, depending on the time of the day and her mind. He suddenly wanted to know her again.

A thousand reasons why he shouldn't call raced through his mind, but one reason to call stuck. Trina Crawford couldn't think of a serious relationship right now, and for what he had in mind, it would only be temporary. Right now, he'd just invite her to have coffee.

He logged onto his laptop and visited her website, filled out the forms and submitted a photo.

Why not support the cause? That might make her more amenable to his situation.

Another idea struck him and he tapped on the keys and pulled up the classmate directory. He dialed the last known number listed for her and waited.

What was the worst that could happen by contacting her and asking if she would help him? She could say no. She'd done that in front of forty thousand people. He hoped she was fresh out of rejection.

Chapter 3

"Did you have to stay for the game? I mean, was that totally humiliating to Drake, or what?"

Astounded, Trina watched her pregnant cousin Shayla Crawford-Parker suck down her second cup of Jell-O. She acted like the baby she was carrying was training to be a pro wrestler before it left the womb.

"I was there for the game, not the proposals from Drake. Why should I have left?"

"It just looked funny that you stayed," her other cousin Trisha pointed out as she laid on the chaise lounge, her sister Tracey sitting quietly on the floor, staring out the window.

Trina loved her bedroom decorated in warm yellows, white, and tans. The accents were an orange pillow here and there, lavender and taupe. Every morning she opened her eyes to the beauty of the sun and it made her feel alive. Drake had hated it and now she was glad she hadn't changed anything. With him out of her life, she could do things her way all the time.

"We're getting ready to have dinner. It's almost done. Do you have to keep eating?" Trina asked, eyeing the bag of popcorn and chips Shayla had finished not a half hour ago.

"Keep it up with the cute remarks, and I'll go make some pork chops and show you how I can get down, okay? Besides, you're supposed to be nice to me. I'm in Atlanta for some much needed R&R. My sweetie thought I'd rest better here than in Mississippi because . . . I'm driving him crazy. Whatever," Shayla sniped, scraping the bottom of the cup with her spoon.

Dropping the cup in the garbage can, Shayla reclaimed her seat. "I guess I did get a little crazy. This bag of snacks was supposed to last a few days. Seven more weeks. Good gracious. I won't make it. Anyway, where's Nona? She's usually in on our girl time."

"She quit. Just walked out and didn't come back. I hate when people do that," Tracey said and they all turned slowly to look at her.

Tracey was the oldest of all the cousins at thirty-one. She'd been going through a bad spell, battling depression. Trina was glad to see her. Tracey had been out of work for a week last month, but had come back. But she'd taken Nona's quitting hard. Especially since Nona had been the office manager of Suddenlysingleatl.com.

Tracey had agreed to handle all the administrative tasks, while her sister Trisha, younger than her by one year, handled advertising.

Shayla looked at Trina. Younger than them all at twenty-nine, she was the dynamo. Pregnant, managing two medical offices, while still seeing patients even in her last trimester, Shayla had energy to burn. "What happened to Nona? Why'd she quit?"

"I don't know," Trina said. "I tried to call her and she wouldn't answer. So I called her from my mother's private line one day and she finally answered. I asked her what was up and she said she was tired of being my springboard."

"What did she mean by that?" Trisha asked, filing her nails, keeping an eye on her twin.

"I asked and she said she didn't owe me an explanation about anything. She had major attitude and so I wasn't anxious to get into it with her."

"Sounds like sour grapes," Shayla said. "I hope she didn't take anything from the company."

Shayla looked at Tracey and Trisha. "I can't be sure. We trusted each other," Trina said, feeling uncomfortable that she hadn't thought of this before.

"That's stupid. I should have known," Tracey said. "She's been acting funny. Oh, never mind."

She got up and walked to the window in the farthest corner in the room.

Trisha bent her head, looked at Trina and Shayla and mouthed, "Help me."

"Tracey? What's wrong? I can't help but see that you're depressed," Shayla said.

She rubbed the back of her neck and rocked on her heel. "Yeah, well. A little. I'll be fine."

"Come here."

"You're not my doctor, Shayla."

"Come here," Shayla said again, softer. "Come on."

Tracey came back and sat between Shayla and Trina on the bed.

They both put their arms around her and Tracey rested her head on Shayla's shoulder.

"Come on. Tell us. We'll help you," Shayla said.

"No. I have to figure it out for myself."

Trisha came over and touched her sister's chin and made her look up. "You are loved. Don't wait too long. You hear me?"

"Yes," she said as sad tears streaked her cheeks.

"Tell me, little sis. What's up? You pregnant?"

"No. I'll get better, Trisha. I'm working it out. I promise."

Trina was concerned and wanted to cry, too. Her cousin was in major pain, but something held her back from telling them. Trina wanted to press Tracey, but Trisha kissed her twin's forehead, letting the matter drop. "Okay," she said, "I'm going to check the food to make sure it doesn't burn."

Trisha rushed out and Trina knew she didn't want to cry in front of Tracey.

Tracey resumed her position by the window and Shayla held up a warning hand and shook her head at Trina who wanted to press the matter.

Trina backed down, while Shayla reached inside her purse and pulled out a solid stick of vitamin E and began to rub it on her belly to prevent stretch marks.

Trina was speechless.

"There's something strangely impersonal

about having a baby, and I think I'm looking at it," Tracey commented, shaking her head, her hand shielding her teary eyes.

They all laughed.

Shayla had been right, Trina acknowledged. This was the old Tracey.

"You've never been in the labor and delivery room. I'm tame," Shayla said, holding her stomach. "But we're not here to talk about me. We're here to talk about Trina and the way she treated Drake." Shayla huffed and puffed and Trina and Tracey helped her stand up.

"Trina, I'd like to point out that Drake has been around the family for a long time, and if you wanted to end your relationship, it would have been nice if you hadn't chosen the arena and a bazillion strangers to do it in front of. Hint, darlin'. Try the phone. It works wonders."

"I agree, but opportunity was kneeling on the floor. I couldn't very well say, 'I know I've told you before that I don't want to get married, but I'm going to wait for a more personal moment so I don't humiliate you in front of strangers.' He started it," Trina pointed out, anger heating her voice. She ran her fingers through her curls and, though frustrated, still loved her shorter hair.

"She's right. How was she to know?" Tracey, who was older than her by four days, weighed in with her dull-toned voice. "Waiting would have only delayed the inevitable. People would have booed her for not making a decision. It looked bad, but she did Drake and herself a favor."

Trisha walked back in. "Ten minutes on

dinner, and getting rid of Drake was good for us in one regard."

Nobody in the room looked convinced, Trina thought. "How do you figure?"

"Did a lot of people register at Suddenlysingleatl.com?" Shayla asked, rubbing her lower back.

"Twenty-five hundred last night alone," Tracey commented. "The more the clip is played on TV, the more people sign up."

Trina held up her hands, frustrated that her personal life had become news fodder. "I don't know why he tried to force my hand. He kept talking about building empires with the Crawfords. He didn't want me. He wanted *us*."

"Honey, this wasn't your fault, I agree," Trisha said, twisting her long hair.

Although Trisha and Tracey were twins, they were as different as night and day. Trisha was always on the go, seeing the big picture, and Tracey was methodical and detail oriented. They'd each kept their hair long and shared the family gene of gray eyes.

They were a striking foursome, Trina thought. Trisha took a seat on the chaise lounge, tucked her feet under her, and thumbed through the hair magazine. She began to twist her hair like the woman in the photo.

"Drake deserved everything he got." Tracey sounded detached. "He was trying to back Trina into a corner. That's why he proposed in front of the entire world. He hedged his bets and thought she wouldn't say no. Trina called his bluff. I need a cigarette."

Trisha gave her a stick of Nicorette gum and went back to twisting her hair.

Trina started straightening up her already neat night table. "You've got one thing wrong," Trina confessed. "I almost said yes."

All of her cousins faced her.

Shayla, the only married woman in the room, held up the hand weighed down by a three-carat diamond ring. "What happened? Why'd you say no?"

"Everyone else in the family *is* married or just about there. I thought maybe if I said yes, I'd suddenly get excited."

"That's the stupidest thing I've ever heard," Tracey said, staring at Trina, her eyes filled with tears. "You're not desperate, so why would you consider doing something so serious without real love?"

"Tracey, I didn't do it. You saw me turn him down. What's gotten into you?"

"Nothing! Think! Isn't Daddy always harping on us about thinking first? Look, I've got to go. I've got laundry to wash and work to do."

Trina reached for her cousin's hand. "Wait, girl. Calm down, sweetie. Don't leave. Please tell us what's wrong."

"Drake is a nice guy, but you're the most important person to us. Don't do something just because you think it's time. We've all been in positions where we could have made major mistakes. But not because we felt left out."

"We're a team," Trisha said, supporting her sister.

Trina nodded, her heart full. "Okay. I have another confession to make."

They'd all inherited their gray-eyed gene from their fathers and it was piercing and direct.

"Are you gay?" Tracey asked.

"What?" Trina flinched, startled at the question out of left field.

"It would stand to reason that one of us would be. There's so many of us. We'd still love you," Tracey assured Trina.

"No, I'm not gay. But, thank you. The truth is I'm not sure I ever want to get married."

Her cousins looked at her as if she'd announced she were going to live on an uninhabited island.

"What did you say?" Trisha moved closer to Trina. "Is it because of Suddenlysingleatl.com? People own businesses and have families," she pointed out. "It's not an all or nothing world out there."

"Wait, I'm confused," Tracey cut in. "You were going to say yes to Drake, and now you're not sure you ever want to get married. Which is it?"

"It was both until I said no. I like my life and when he was pressuring me, I almost said yes, but then I realized I don't *have* to have a man. Drake was a good guy, but I don't have to get married and that's what he was trying to force me to do. Once I said no, I felt immense relief. Drake wants a business merger. Before we got on TV, he was talking about an alliance between the families, and I felt like he was using me."

"I don't know that I want to have children," Trina said.

"Don't ever let Mama hear you say that," Trisha said in a hushed tone. "She might perform an exorcism."

Her cousins laughed, but Trina could tell they were troubled. The women in her family were trained to want their own families. She was bucking tradition. In essence, she was bucking them.

"Listen, I love the family, but I just don't know that I want the whole shebang myself."

"Now?" Shayla asked, massaging her belly protectively.

"Or forever?" Trisha finished the sentence they all wanted answered.

"For—" Trina's cell phone rang. "Trina Crawford."

"This is Reno Merriwether from UGA. How are you?"

"Reno. Oh my goodness, it's been forever."

Finishing the word she'd begun seconds ago, Trina looked back at Shayla. Rejection and hurt glowed in her eyes, followed by a small forgiving smile. Who wouldn't want to be a part of them?

Shayla had come into the family practically as an adult, was now comfortably a Crawford, and would be adding a new one soon.

"Reno, it's been too long. How'd you get my number?"

"Your mother gave it to me."

Trina couldn't help smiling at the sound of his voice. All those years ago, she'd reacted the same way. "Of course mom gave it to you."

"Is that okay?"

"Yes!" She checked the excitement in her voice. "Yes, it's just that my cousins are here and we were just about to sit down to dinner. Girls, Reno Merriwether from UGA. Remember him?"

"Hey Reno," they all sang, then giggled.

Trina squinted at them, and they giggled some more.

"I don't want to interrupt your dinner, but I'd love to catch up. Do you think you can fit me into your schedule for coffee tomorrow?"

"Coffee tomorrow?" Trina looked at her cousins, who resembled bobblehead dolls. "Let's say 10:30. At Café Intermezzo on Peachtree?"

"Intermezzo? Sounds nice and fancy," he said, a smile in his voice, which only made her wonder what he looked like after all this time. "Sounds like a winner to me. 10:30 is perfect."

"Reno, how will I know you?"

"I look the same, just a few years older."

"I do, too," Trina added.

"I know. I saw you on the game."

"Oh my goodness. Not my finest hour."

"Fine you were indeed," he said.

"You didn't have to say that, but thank you. Okay, Reno. Tomorrow."

Trina sat next to Shayla who'd temporarily stopped chewing. Her gaze was probing. "Trina, may I say one thing?" she finally said.

"Sure."

Shayla and her mother Lauren had proved to be tremendous advocates for women in Georgia and Mississippi. They'd begun programs to help single moms and their children learn job skills that were hugely successful. If Shayla had wisdom to share, Trina was willing to listen.

"I don't think Drake was right for you. After watching you just now on the phone with Mr. Man from the past, Drake should be history. Give Reno a chance."

Trina crossed and uncrossed her legs. "Honey, please. We're two old friends reconnecting. It's been about eight years. It'll be fun to see him again."

"She's got a point." Trisha chewed a piece of Tracey's Nicorette gum, then spit it out. "Yuck!"

"It's not for you. Silly." Tracey took the gum from her twin's palm and threw it away before giving her a piece of sugar-free gum from her purse.

"You two are ridiculous. Why don't you carry your own gum? If I get my hands on those purses, out the window they go," Shayla said, half-serious.

"Your husband is so glad you're gone," Trisha said and they all laughed.

"Let's eat and then you can tell me all about Mr. Merriwether," Shayla said.

Trina escorted her cousins to the kitchen and fixed plates of greens, cornbread, salmon, baked chicken, green beans, potato salad, and pineapple upside down cake.

They all sat down to eat on the heated screened in porch. "Reno was my first love." Trina rubbed her chest over her heart. "He was pretty special."

"What did he look like?" Shayla dug into her Louis Vuitton satchel for her cell phone. Trina admired the bag, having two of her own, but she still wanted Shayla's.

"He was a handsome man. Tall, brown skin, with a sexy deep voice that could ripple a sidewalk."

"Like my Jake," Shayla said.

"Sort of," Trisha agreed. "Only more aggressive and cuter."

"Taller," Trina supplied. "Dimples. No bucked teeth, either."

"Hey," Shayla pouted. "Jake's teeth aren't bucked."

The girls stopped teasing Shayla and giggled.

"You three are just jealous because Jake is so wonderful. "What ended things between you and Reno?" she wondered.

"He wanted to transfer to Michigan State his senior year, my junior, and I didn't want to leave UGA. We decided we didn't want to do the long-distance thing, so we broke up and promised not to keep in touch."

"Sick," Trisha whispered.

Shayla and Tracey agreed.

Trina chuckled. "It was very mature of us. Everybody else was walking around with broken hearts and we were the only mature people free to date and go on with our lives without the drama. So that's what we did. Tomorrow we'll be two old friends catching up."

"Keep saying it and maybe you'll start believing it, because I don't." Trisha stretched and yawned.

"It's a no-pressure situation," Shayla said diplomatically. "A little coffee, talking, and who knows?"

"Personally, I don't know why you're going," Tracey said, her low mood moving around them like a fog. "You already said you're not interested in getting married or having babies. Why waste the man's time?"

"Tracey," Trisha admonished. "Do you have to yank on the string of your rain cloud every chance you get?"

"Sorry. But Reno's still available, right?" Tracey asked.

"I couldn't tell just by saying hi," Trina told her.

"It's going to fail, you know. It's a consummate rebound relationship for you," Tracey predicted.

Trisha got her coat and sighed loudly. "I'm leaving," she announced, mouthing, "Sorry," to Trina.

Tracey dragged her coat halfway up her arm. When it snagged on her sweater, she gave up, leaving it half rolled.

Shayla put her hands on Tracey's arms, letting her know to stop struggling, then she gently pulled the sleeves down. Tracey then shrugged right into the coat.

"I've got a long day ahead of me tomorrow. We're still going for that Small Business Organization Contest, right?" she said to Trina.

"Definitely. Our application for the contest has to be in by Friday and I'm almost done with it. We'll be ready." Trina reached out and hugged her. "Goodnight, Tracey. Night, Trisha."

"Night, girls." Trina closed the door softly and

watched Trisha and Tracey get into their cars and drive away.

"Shayla, do you think Tracey could use an antidepressant?"

"Definitely, but I'm just her cousin, not her doctor."

"Can't you do anything?"

"I'm here, aren't I?"

Trina's mouth fell open. "That's why you're here. I should have known Jake wouldn't let you out of his sight this late in your pregnancy. You're here because of Tracey. Who asked you? Was there a summit meeting of the family and I wasn't involved?"

"No. Trisha called and said she thought if we got together for dinner, I could diagnose Tracey's condition. She's definitely sad, but without a thorough evaluation, I can't give a diagnosis. This may all have to do with her quitting smoking."

Trina started filling the dishwasher. "She just quit and she's been depressed for about a month. Something's going on with her."

"One thing I've learned about you Crawfords—"

"Excuse me?" Trina said, playfully indignant.

"*Us* Crawfords," Shayla corrected. "When we get ready for everyone to know something, they'll know. I'd better get going. Baby brother is just six, but he wants his big sister to sleep in his room."

"Sucker," Trina quipped. "You, in a twin bunk bed? That's funny."

"Only part of the night. When he dozes off

I'll go to my room. Any idea what you're wearing tomorrow?"

"I'm thinking jeans, cute black top." Trina finished the top rack and loaded the plates in record time.

"Wear the jeans I gave you last Christmas, Trina. They're tight and sexy."

"I'll wear my old Levi's, thanks."

"Those babe magnets," Shayla said facetiously. "Wow." Shayla started the Roomba vacuum cleaner and wiped off the kitchen table just as Trina closed the dishwasher door and started the machine.

Trina followed her cousin up the hallway and helped her with her coat. "Shayla, I'm not trying to catch a babe. I'm going out of curiosity mostly. You know, I was part of a couple for so long, I want to see if there's any . . ."

Shayla took Trina by the shoulders. "Attraction. I get it. Drake's history. Look, it's too soon to be making a decision about dating and marrying someone else. Go have coffee in your Levi's and have fun. That's all that matters, and a call to me with a detailed report when it's over."

Trina nodded. Moments ago she'd been afraid to tell her cousins her deepest feelings, but now she didn't want Shayla to leave.

Shayla must have sensed her pensive mood. "Hey, you going to be all right? Maybe it's too soon."

"No, I'm fine. Sometimes I wish I was a kid again. Go back to a time when we didn't have adult worries."

Shayla stuck her tongue in her cheek. "Honey, no way. I'm having more fun as an adult."

Trina gazed at her. "You are?"

"Yes, honey. I couldn't have sex as a child."

Trina laughed and kissed her cousin's cheek. "Night, crazy Shayla."

"Night, baby doll. Call me."

"I will," Trina said.

As soon as she closed the door, she hurried to her closet and began the predate ritual, a whole twenty hours early.

Trina tried to talk herself out of it, but couldn't stop from reaching for the Seven jeans Shayla had given her. They fit like a glove and she loved them, but telling Shayla would have inflated her ego.

Trina pulled down her favorite black top, then boots from the bottom row of boxes and a belt from the corner spinner. Next came a variety of purses until she settled on a wristlet. Laying the clothes on the chaise lounge, she took her shower and dressed for bed.

She glanced at the clothes before turning her attention to the application she was supposed to finish. Forcing her thoughts on the questions, Trina consulted her tax returns and filled in the appropriate boxes, keeping her mind away from the Reno she once knew.

He'd been a tough guy in college. He'd been all muscular on the basketball team, but he was a teddy bear with her.

Trina had liked that about him. The duo personality thing had worked for them until one day he'd used it against her and told her he was leaving UGA for Michigan State and their relationship was over.

She'd put up a brave front, but Reno had torn her heart to shreds. If she wasn't careful, he'd get another chance.

But she wasn't going there. She was going to find out what had happened that fateful day, and then she was going to put that day along with all the other days of her past to rest.

Chapter 4

Reno stood in his bedroom adjusting his watch, but could hear Chloe's agonizing struggle with Mrs. Teralyn as she battled to leave the woman's arms to come with him. She didn't cry out, but grunted as she pushed and pulled and fought to get out of her arms. He'd tried to leave while she'd been asleep, but she must have sensed him leaving because she'd appeared in the doorway of his office with June tucked under her left arm and her coat in her right hand.

She'd put on pink Capri pants from last summer and had stuffed her feet into her favorite too-small red patent leather shoes. Her hair was wild and her beautiful chocolate kiss-colored cheek was creased where she'd slept hard on the sheet.

He knew his right eyebrow had shot up because hers did, too. He'd adopted this precious child, but she was so much a part of him they could have been blood of blood. Her face was full of sleep and she hadn't eaten, but she knew her daddy was going out.

"Chloe, you're going to stay here with Mrs. Teralyn," he said from his room while they were in the hallway. "She's going to watch you while I go to a meeting. Then you and I will have lunch, and school and work in daddy's office."

She hadn't bought it then and she wasn't buying it now.

She was struggling harder, fighting, but she didn't cry out, she just fought for him. How could he bear to leave her?

For a minute the hallway was silent, so he took that as his sign to exit. He thought they'd gone out on the patio, but didn't check. Mrs. Teralyn was good at clearing a path for him, but he still hated that Chloe was upset.

At the car door, he heard her struggling vigorously and Reno turned and took the garage stairs in one leap and was back in the kitchen. He and Chloe reached for each other simultaneously. The little girl plastered herself to his chest and he rubbed her back, her heart racing. Her face was buried in his shirt, her little hands stretched around his neck. "It's all right, baby. It's all right. Daddy's here."

"You two did better," Mrs. Teralyn said softly. "Four minutes this time. It's better when you leave when she's asleep."

Reno felt as if he'd run a marathon, his own heart beating hard. How was he going to meet Trina with Chloe along? He could reschedule, but he didn't want to.

"Mrs. Teralyn, do you feel up to a field trip?"

The grandmother of ten scurried off to get her coat and was back with a few toys. "Let's go."

Reno sat at one table, unsure if he'd chosen a good seat. He loved Café Intermezzo. The dessert bar, a tall glass-enclosed case of decadent delights of pies and cakes, was magnificent, but was surpassed by the extensive international menu of coffee and teas. He sat alone and for a few minutes, let his body equalize. He was rarely a single man. He was always a single father. Always a businessman. Never just Reno.

Chloe had fallen asleep on the ride over, which surprised him, but he was thankful for small favors. He'd pay for it later. She'd be up all night. Mrs. Teralyn had spied a whimsical children's store next door she'd try to distract Chloe with, but Reno knew he didn't have the luxury of a lot of time.

Chloe needed him.

Reno walked the entire restaurant again, and then chose a seat facing the door on the right side of the restaurant so he could see Trina's approach and entrance. Folding his hands, then opening them again, he wiped them on his jeans, glancing out the window, when he saw a woman walking down Peachtree Street.

She strode down the sidewalk clad in nice jeans, a camel-colored leather jacket, multicolored scarf around her neck, her booted feet gliding over the uneven pavement. She stopped at the corner, her hand resting atop a long multicolored umbrella as a car rolled to a stop in front of her.

Absently, she smoothed hair that wasn't there behind her ear. She must have just cut it. He thought the cute curls were perfect for her.

He spied shamelessly on Trina as she crossed. Then the driver rolled down his window and said something. Trina turned around and offered him a flirtatious smile, but declined whatever offer he'd made. She entered the restaurant long before the man ever drove off. She still had that effect on men.

Reno stood up and she saw him. For the second time that day, his heart pounded.

"Reno Merriwether. My goodness. You do look the same."

"Trina."

Her name rolled from him like a long slow sigh. She'd extended her hand, but he'd already moved to wrap her in a warm embrace. The fact that he'd surprised her didn't bother Reno. She didn't pull away. For that he was glad.

Someone behind them cleared his throat but Reno wasn't about to let go. "This is a reunion," he said over his shoulder. "We might be a minute."

"That's okay." Trina laughed and broke the embrace. She looked away nervously and began to unzip her jacket.

"Is this table good for you?" Reno asked. "We can sit somewhere else if you'd like." He felt like a teenager again, wanting to treat Atlanta's royalty to the best.

"What better place than right across from the dessert bar? We've got the best seats in the house."

Her jacket went over the back of the chair with practiced ease and she crossed her legs while playing with her earring. He remembered that nervous gesture and how she used to strum her fingers on any flat surface when she was flustered.

Why would Trina be nervous? This was the restaurant of her choosing. Her town. Her life.

She looked more beautiful than he remembered, smelled like lavender, and she'd felt so good he wouldn't soon forget holding her.

"I've never been here before. How'd you know about this place?"

"Atlanta has lots of little treasures like Intermezzo."

"You'll have to share them with me. This is very nice."

The waitress recognized Trina and spoke to her in French. Trina responded, her face lighting up. She ordered Vienna coffee and turned to Reno.

He had no idea what she'd said. "I'll have what she's having."

They both laughed. "Smart man," the waitress said and walked away.

"You speak French now."

"An acquired language when you spend three summers in France."

"Ah. Usted habla Español?" he said, asking if she spoke Spanish.

"Si, Reno. Como esta usted?" she said, inquiring how he was.

"Bien, bella."

"Fine, beautiful. Wow, you're still a flirt. But enough Spanish," Trina said. Settling back in her chair, Trina crossed her legs and pushed her hands between her knees. "Reno?"

He liked the way she said his name. For the first time in a long time, being single had its benefits. "Yes?"

"Why did you call me?"

Reno sat back and drank in the sight of her. Confidence curved her back and made it look sexy. Her lips curled over pretty white teeth, and God had given her the best come-hither gaze he'd seen on a woman in years. "Reno? The reason for your call?" she said again.

"Well, I saw you on TV."

"I know. I've gotten more calls than I care to think about regarding my unfortunate television debut."

He nodded, propelling himself and his thoughts forward. "I thought, 'How'd she get tickets to the game?'"

Trina laughed and the nervousness seemed to fly away from her.

"Now that's a new one. Well, they're family seats," she finally said. Trina shrugged carelessly. She was a woman who enjoyed her life and its perks. "We could catch a game sometime. But, I have to say, I just don't see you calling me to score basketball tickets."

She purposely looked him up and down. "You're dressed not too shabbily. The Hugo Boss leather jacket is very nice. You have on a Seiko watch, and your shoes are shined." Her gaze took the long route up to his. "All the superficial bases are covered. So, the question from all my cousins will be what did he really want? Is he married?"

"Second question first. I was. Not anymore."

"But you still feel married."

"Definitely not."

She leaned forward and he liked that she was interested. "Why are we here?"

"Why'd you say no to him?"

Reno expected Trina to resist his abrupt invasion in her privacy. Being old friends didn't grant him or anyone access. But after the game debacle, perhaps private had taken on new perspectives. He just hoped she didn't mind because he needed to know.

"I don't want to get married. Period."

His stomach knotted at her crisp, clear response, but he didn't react outwardly. There had to be an underlying reason for her adamant stance, and he intended to get to the bottom of it and turn her objection around, if only for a short time.

Their drinks and food arrived, and Reno found them facing a very large piece of red velvet cake for two. The server provided two forks and walked off.

Picking up their forks, they eyed each other tentatively.

Once upon a time, they'd shared every intimacy. Now a piece of cake had them acting like shy teenagers.

Trina's smile radiated to her eyes. Then an ignition switch inside flipped. The impersonal glow of interest between two old friends shifted into the realm of "what if."

Reno's heart celebrated with a little, Bring in

da Stomp, but he cautioned himself to take it slow.

Looking at the cake he said, "This is good."

"You haven't even tasted it." Their forks met and she pulled hers away and ate.

"I know. Dessert before lunch. I love it. Why?"

"Life doesn't always have to follow a plan. When you're an adult you can do anything you want, when you want."

"There's probably about thirty million people in the world who are at jobs they hate and would disagree with you."

"It works for me."

"Except for marriage," he said, digging.

"I'm not opposed to it for the entire world. Just for me. Single is good enough for me."

"Single," Reno said, swallowing the cake, loving the coffee, hating the conversation.

"After the basketball game I found myself suddenly single, and to be honest, I'm loving it."

"You weren't hurt?"

"I miss being part of a couple, but I've been single for just a little while. I'll get over that," she said softly.

On that Reno understood her well. He hated that he often started to speak and there was no one to hear him. At least when he'd been married he and his wife had occasional conversations.

But it wasn't loneliness he fought anymore. Time was his worst enemy now.

"Tell me about your business," he said, hoping to delay her curiosity about why they were there.

"It's called Suddenlysingleatl.com and it's a dotcom dating service. Singles sign up to meet one another. They complete a profile and a personality test. Then the computer matches them with other compatible singles."

"I thought they could choose themselves."

"They can. You've been to the site." She seemed genuinely surprised.

"I'm a member."

Reno appreciated every elegant yet nervous move she made. Her fingers drummed against the table. "Don't keep me in suspense. What do you like?"

"It's a good site. I like that a headshot is required for every person who joins."

"It's only fair," Trina said. "I don't want it to be a hotbed for extramarital affairs. I did extensive research and found a lot of other sites out there for that."

"It's good to have standards."

"Those sites have far better numbers than Suddenlysingleatl."

"But you're new. If you want to get into a larger arena later, you can. I like that it's required to answer the profile and personality test."

"Okay, give me the negatives," she said, but only after she clenched her hand by her cheek into a tight fist.

"Why are you asking me to do this?"

"You have nothing to lose by being honest. We're old friends and you're a fresh perspective."

"Okay, but you asked. Remember that."

"I never remember you stalling so much. We'd have never won a championship with you acting this way."

Reno folded his arms, liking her upfront

personality couched in femininity. "Too many
obstacles in the beginning. If two adults want to
meet or exchange numbers, why make them go
through a week of back and forth on the site?"

"They should be sure they want to meet the
other person by finding out as much as possible.
You know how it is. Something looks real good,
but the more you hear, the less you like. We're
trying to weed out undesirables on both sides."

Reno shrugged. "That's smart, but it could be
a nuisance when you think you've met the right
person, and you don't have the freedom to talk."

"It's for safety, too, but," Trina massaged her
shoulders, a job Reno found himself wanting.
"Maybe we can offer a speedway-type process for
people who immediately meet certain criteria.
The focus groups liked the current set up best.
So we went with it."

"Some things can't be quantified, Trina. Like
emotion."

An expression passed over Trina's face, but
she immediately looked out the window, then
back at him. Her features had smoothed and the
storm that seemed to bother her had passed.
"We want the referrals, too. The longer a person
visits the site, the more they tell friends about
their success."

"True, but if the brotha isn't worth her time,
why make her wait two weeks to find out? An upfront conversation can answer a lot of questions
and both parties can move on."

Something he said hit home. Her cheeks had
turned pink.

"Want to talk about it?"

"No." Trina waved her hands. "I got a similar lecture from my cousin Shayla. Maybe we'll try it that way and see how it goes. We also discourage more than two at a time."

"Why," Reno asked, wondering if one woman would be enough for him. The right woman would. "If marriage isn't the goal, why do you care how many people they date?"

"I guess," she started, then drummed her fingers on the table, dragging them in slow circles.

Reno gazed at her. He didn't mean to compare Trina with Dana, but his ex never asked him for advice.

Trina pulled a BlackBerry from her bag and took notes. "You're right. We're not like other sites. We're not in the marriage business. We're in the dating business, and I shouldn't forget that." Trina laughed and patted his arm. "I've got several events planned. What do you think of a night at the High Museum or the Aquarium? An evening at the Hawks game or movie night at the park?"

"I like all of them. But don't you have any disorganized fun?"

Trina looked beautifully confused.

"A picnic. No walking in a line for a ticket, no getting dressed up. Just having fun at the park."

"We might be able to manage that. We only have to have four events. What else?"

Reno didn't know why he was enjoying himself so much. He had lunch weekly with clients and monthly with friends, but this was different. "Are you positive?" he asked.

"Go for it. You've given me a lot to think about."

"My last suggestion is to show the pictures gallery style. As for increasing traffic, we can save that topic for another date."

"How do you know there'll be another date?"

"A man can dream," he said, hoping to coax a smile from her. "The site is good. I've met a woman. She's interesting."

Reno watched Trina pantomime her nervousness.

"Interesting in a good way or get-a-restraining-order interesting?"

"Nothing like that," he chuckled, eating more cake. "I like her. I hope she likes me."

"Really! Oh. Well."

Why was he pleased that she sounded faintly jealous?

"How will your company be different from others?"

"We're planning local events based upon membership. The big thing is that I just entered an entrepreneurial contest. If we're successful, we could win $250,000."

"We?"

"Investors and I."

"I see. Which contest? I did one a couple years ago."

"Small Business Opportunities Corporation."

Reno sat back and crossed his arms. "I won that contest three years ago. That's how I launched my business."

Trina's gray eyes sparkled. "I had no idea.

What do you do, Reno? We've been talking all this time about me and I never even asked."

"I own a consulting company. We specialize in garbage disposal and recycling."

Her eyebrows crinkled. "You dispose of trash?"

He nodded. "That's right. You can't bury it all so my specialty is reusing it. I just won a contract with the two largest cities in Africa on reusing plastic and aluminum."

"Wow. That's so—"

"Boring, I know. I've heard that before."

"Interesting. How did you go from getting a degree in communication to recycling materials?"

"I started at a company in finance. I thought I would eventually go into public relations, but found myself interested in how we can use recycled materials in our everyday lives. I also had ideas about how to grow the company. But I held on to them and when the owner retired, I bought him out. So here I am."

"That's very noble work. I feel silly talking about dotcom dating."

Red velvet cake got stuck in his throat because she'd reached across the table and was stroking his hand. He moved and she realized what she'd been doing and drew back.

"You're doing the world a great service, be-lieve me," he told her when he could speak again. "When people aren't happy, well, you see the world we live in."

Trina rolled her eyes. Still a smile tugged at her lips. "I doubt dating can be credited with saving the powers that be from themselves."

Reno cut the remainder of the cake in half,

but she'd long ago set down her fork. "I don't know. Make love not war," he said.

A surprised burst of laughter shot from her. "What the hell are you talking about?" she asked, kidding him.

"My father used to say that when Dana and I would argue."

"Your ex."

"Yeah. How's your family?" he asked.

"Everybody's fine," she said, looking as if she were ready to side-step any talk about them. "Reno, I'd welcome any tips you could give me on my business plan. I've read the rules. There's nothing saying we can't get advice."

He remembered coaching Trina to her second slam dunk and welcomed the opportunity to do it again. "Definitely. I got an e-mail about the upcoming launch reception, but hadn't planned to go. I'll reconsider now that I know you're going to be there."

"It'll be nice to see a friendly face."

"Not to change the subject," he said, "but you might be interested to know I had one perfect match on your site. All ten stars with just one woman."

She relaxed, letting herself be sucked into the matrix of her own dream. "You should have told me. What's she like? Is she cute? Nice? Have you met her yet?"

"Eat this last little bit of cake with me and I'll tell you about her."

She seemed to consider his offer for a moment, then picked up her fork. "Okay, but then I have to get going. Tell me about her."

"She's you."

Trina had stuck the fork into her mouth and slowly withdrew it. "Reno, you and I were a long time ago. I just ended one relationship. You saw it." Her mouth moved into a sad smile. "I'm not ready to be with anyone and I'm going to shoot Tracey."

"Your cousin? Why?"

"Now that I think about it, this isn't Tracey's style. But Trisha, she's a regular buttinsky. She put my profile on the site and made it seem like I was available."

"Well, you asked the real reason I contacted you. I have a business proposition. A proposal."

The waitress dropped the check on the table and moved on to help another table of customers.

Reno saw Chloe the moment she entered the restaurant and wished for the first time his daughter had better timing. Or at least looked better. Those hot pink capris and the too small red patent leather shoes weren't ever going to make the perfect outfit, unless you were four-years old.

Reno hadn't mentioned Chloe to Trina, because if she wasn't thinking marriage, she definitely wasn't thinking children.

But Chloe, being four, didn't think. She acted. She saw her daddy and flew into his lap.

Trina blinked rapidly.

Reno again regretted that their timing wasn't better.

Mrs. Teralyn mouthed her apology, then bustled off in the direction of the ladies' room.

"Trina, this is my daughter Chloe, and she's

partly the reason I need to marry you," he said in Spanish so that Chloe would not understand their conversation.

"There's a bigger reason?"

"She has a sister in Africa, and in order to adopt her, I need to be married."

Trina stood, causing the waitress behind her to veer sharply to the left, making the tray on her right hand waver.

Everyone saw the disaster, but Trina reacted. She steadied the tray with her fingertips and spoke firmly while looking the waitress in the eye. "We're not going to drop it."

You'd have thought she'd spent years in the military. She seemed accustomed to taking charge and diffusing what could have been a disaster.

"If you're ready, I'll give you the tray."

"Ready," the waitress said, pulling herself together.

She delivered the food to the waiting table while the manager gave Trina a silent clap of thanks.

Chloe saw the colored scarf that Trina had worn around her neck and she touched it just as Trina picked it up.

"Thank you," Trina said.

Chloe merely nodded and shrugged.

Trina swept hair that wasn't there back behind her ear and an annoyed expression rippled across her brows, then disappeared. She shook her head without saying a word.

"I know your dotcom is important to you," Reno said softly in Spanish. Chloe stuck her fingers in his mouth because she didn't understand what he was saying. Reno looked down at the girl, kissed her fingers and held them in his hand.

"Trina, I'll help you win the contest. If you help me get her sister. I need your help. *We* need your help. After we get her, you're free. I'll pay you for your time and after the divorce, I'll never bother you again."

Trina looked at the pair. "No," she said and hurried out.

Chapter 5

The announcement of the finalists for the SBO Contest was happening within the next half hour, and Trina would know if her company had made it. She'd dressed for the formal occasion like the other entrants, but she was minus an accessory. She didn't have a man or a family member with her.

For once in her life, Trina was glad none of her fifty million relatives were around, which was odd because she'd always taken great comfort in being a Crawford.

Their name was like reinforced steel in Atlanta. Today she was glad she didn't have to hold it down for all the Crawfords.

She'd told Trisha and Tracey she'd call them with the results, but pleaded that they hold off telling the rest of the family until she got back to the office.

This was her first independent venture. She wanted to win, and to prove she had truly come into her own as a professional.

Two weeks had passed since Suddenlysingle atl.com had been accepted into the contest. Their schedule was now posted on the site, and she'd gotten a call today to finalize the details.

To avoid nervousness, Trina walked the distinguished halls of the Madison Museum, praying that her company would be awarded the opportunity to compete for the $250,000. This was the initial elimination phase, and there were three companies in her category. Only two would compete for the prize.

Tonight she'd meet the other contestants and she'd be gracious, but she'd also size up the competition.

Trina sipped champagne and sat on the edge of a Victorian chair, pressing her body into relaxation mode. She wanted to guzzle the knotty beverage, but decorum dictated a more sophisticated protocol. So she sipped a little more than she ordinarily would have.

Competitors in other divisions mingled in five rooms of the internationally renowned art museum. On display this year was art from the Athenian era, and Trina wished she could have appreciated the beautiful black and red vases from the sixth and fourth centuries. Only one thing in the room captured her attention, however, and it moved and breathed.

As hard as she tried not to be surprised, she was. Reno walked in and women noticed.

He chatted with the contest director, shaking hands with men whom she'd heard of, but didn't know. They were tycoons of their industries, mining for talent in a place where fresh ideas were rewarded.

Reno had won the contest three years ago and had mentioned that he'd received an invitation to tonight's reception, but she didn't know he'd stayed in contact with the people involved. He hadn't mentioned it at lunch a week ago. But then again, they'd only had one lunch, and she hadn't taken his calls since.

It had been seven whole days since she'd seen Reno, but thoughts of him consumed her so badly that she'd taken a tumble while at the gym on the treadmill this morning.

Embarrassed, she'd gotten up and dusted herself off, and accepted the good-natured ribbing from the men that they wanted to be the man in her life. They wouldn't let her fall.

Reno didn't seem like that type either. He'd grown up well, and she could see that he'd turned into a successful businessman and father.

Most of all she couldn't help remembering how well they'd fit sexually. They'd been young, but Reno had known what he was doing.

If age was anything like wine, she could only speculate as to how good he'd gotten.

Even now, at this pivotal moment in her life, she still remembered how his hands had caressed her. How his mouth had claimed her and how he'd coaxed climaxes from her body.

Why had Reno's proposal affected her more than Drake's? Why did she want Reno to know that her refusal of marriage was about fulfilling her goals, and not about rejecting him?

There had been sincerity in his eyes and

truthfulness in his tone, and she knew he wasn't trying to play games.

But surely, as fine and kind as Reno was, he could find someone better suited to be his stand-in wife.

Trina turned away, forcing herself to think of the company and all the events she'd planned. She'd made the changes he had suggested and had seen an increase in enrollment of thirty percent. The man obviously knew his stuff.

A contestant burst out crying, and her husband escorted her from the room. Every once in a while another contestant would crack under the pressure, and Trina's pulse would spike.

Holding her silver clutch, she tried to stay unemotional, but she didn't have the distraction of a family member to talk to, and being alone was getting the best of her. She breathed deeply, holding it for a few beats, then released it.

She was going to lose it.

Trina held her composure and headed for the terrace. Fresh air was the only remedy. Outside, she dropped the pretense of being calm and grabbed the railing, letting her breath come in loud ragged gasps.

She wasn't a real Crawford if she started crying, she thought as tears burned her eyes.

"I'm a smart, savvy entrepreneur, and I deserve the opportunity to prove my business will be successful. I'm going to be fine," she told the stars.

"Don't be nervous," he said in a husky voice.

Startled, Trina gripped the railing harder, as her anxiety tangled with the thrill of hearing Reno's voice.

"It's not nerves." Convincing herself was a harder sell. "I didn't want to do the fifty-yard dash to the powder room, so I came out here to get some air."

"Let me help you." His voice was gentle and appealed to her. But she'd only left a relationship a week ago. How could she possibly be thinking about another man?

She lifted her chin. "No."

All week she'd been contrary at work, and it was because of Reno's reentry into her life. Tracey and Trisha had been tense and yesterday had ordered her home for the rest of the day.

Did she need another intervention?

"How can you help me?"

"No matter what you think, even the indomitable Trina Crawford needs someone sometime. That's why you're here alone, right? You thought you could handle it? It's okay."

Slowly, gently, he kneaded the tension from her back. Her muscles moved under his hands.

Trina slid away. "Sorry, thanks. I just need to get a massage."

"Wasn't that a massage?" he asked, a sexy smile curving his lips.

"By a professional." Her bracelet sparkled from a shaft of light coming from inside the museum.

"I've never gotten such low marks," he said, chuckling.

"I just meant by a masseuse. I'm going to stop talking now. Thanks, really. I should get inside."

"You sure you're okay? I could do the other side." He acted as if he wouldn't mind devoting more of his time to her relaxation needs.

Trina didn't want to embarrass herself by melting off the terrace. "You're really nice, Reno, but no thanks."

Trina hated comparing, but not once during her two-year relationship with Drake had he ever given her a massage.

Trina stepped inside, Reno behind her.

Trina wished she'd prolonged the solitude of the outdoors. Being inside the air-conditioned room gave her that closed up feeling again. "Where's your date?"

Reno leaned down to hear her and she was flattered. She was six-two in heels, so few men were taller than her, but Reno was, by two inches. "She's probably looking high and low for you."

"I didn't bring a date. Why are you here alone?"

"I came alone because if I'm chosen as a finalist, I want to soak it in for about a half-hour, then call my family and share the good news."

"Who will you celebrate with?"

"I'll find someone," she said softly. "Speak your dreams into existence. Remember those words?" she asked him.

Reno hadn't forgotten them. He looked down at the confident woman and liked what he saw. "Well, good luck."

"Thank you."

"If you don't mind, I'll stick around until after your category. Maybe we can have a drink or something?"

"Will all contestants please assemble? It's time to announce the finalists," an announcer said over the museum's intercom system.

"This is the moment you've been waiting for,"

Reno said to Trina as they moved toward the crowd in the room holding the sculptures she'd been admiring earlier. "You're already a winner."

Trina gripped his hands. "Thank you. A drink, later?" she asked as the excitement in the room increased.

"Definitely." Reno released her hands so she could go the rest of the way alone.

"Good evening, I'm Breanna German, chairperson for the SBO Contest. As you all know, the Small Business Opportunity Contest is an opportunity for young entrepreneurs to not only pursue their business dreams, but showcase their talent for the entire state of Georgia.

"Applications were submitted and accepted, but only two contestants will move on to the next round. Each category will have two finalists, so let's begin.

"For the category of dotcom dating there are three entrants. Please step forward when your company is called. Suddenlysingleatl.com. Owner, Trina L. Crawford. Loveandlife.com. Owner, Nona M. Saint. And finally, singleand-free.com. Owner Hedda B. Ford."

Reno watched Trina's face closely. She should have been beaming, but her lips were pressed together in a fake smile. Her hands were folded in front of her, yet an earnest energy surrounded her that hadn't been there before. In fact, when Nona M. Saint stepped back from taking her bow, Trina and Nona exchanged words.

Trina looked angry, and he wondered what was going on. She looked ready to fight in her black dress, crystal shoes, and chandelier earrings. Now that would be interesting.

He let his gaze lock with Trina's. *Relax*, he mouthed.

She gave a short nod.

You're a winner, he thought, trying telepathy to communicate with her.

When he smiled again, a genuine smile came back.

Mrs. German accepted an envelope from her assistant.

"Please step forward when your name is called," Mrs. German said. "The first finalist in the dotcom dating division is Suddenlysingleatl.com, owner Trina L. Crawford!"

Trina stepped forward and waved, then returned to her original position.

For all her hard work she didn't linger in the spotlight, but accepted her few seconds and stepped back. She was already preparing her next steps.

Trina was looking for him and he waved. She gave him a silent thank you.

He accepted, putting his hand to his chest then extending it to her.

"The second finalist is Loveandlife.com, owner Nona M. Saint. Congratulations!"

Nona bumped Trina's arm on her way forward. The brush of disrespect was calculated.

With the spotlight hers, Nona put on a show of screams and leaps for her finalist status.

Mrs. German's disappointment was obvious. "Please join me in thanking all of our contestants."

Trina shook Hedda's hand, displaying more

class than Nona, who was still basking in her fading spotlight. By the time she finished jumping around, Trina had shaken hands with all the judges.

Mrs. German tapped the microphone. "Will both finalists please join me for a moment? I must say it's a rare yet welcome day to see young women blazing trails in the dotcom business. Good luck to both of you. You may rejoin your family and friends, but please don't leave. We have envelopes with new instructions for the remainder of the contest."

Trina stalked through the crowd until she found Reno. "I need to see you, please."

"I need a minute. Where will you be?"

"The Sahara room."

He followed, but held back and watched Nona. She slipped from the main room, into a smaller one with a handsomely dressed woman and a cameraman. Trina's ex, Drake, who apparently was there as Nona's date, joined the women.

Reno stood outside the door, out of view and overheard Nona bragging about how she'd always dreamed of starting an online dating company in Atlanta. Entering the contest would allow her to showcase her talent for business and allow her to get the recognition she deserved.

Nona explained that she and Trina had been best friends, but that didn't give the entitled Princess Crawford the right to muscle in on Nona's success. She told the reporter that Trina was trying to steal the $250,000 in winnings, and she wasn't having it.

Although Trina had been *her* former employer,

Nona didn't have a problem viewing her as a hostile competitor, and she would beat Trina Crawford fair and square.

Reno refused to believe Trina would steal anything from anyone. She didn't have to. Besides, he'd seen how receptive she was to new ideas.

Trina wasn't stealing anything. She was still finding her way.

Nona went on to list her upcoming events and promised those who signed up with her company nice gifts from her family's exclusive watch business. She ended by issuing a challenge to Trina to post her event schedule online to show everyone that she was a thief.

The interviewer asked Drake a question, but Reno had heard enough. These two deserved each other.

He strolled down the long hallway, contemplating how he could help Trina, when he noticed a familiar arm wave him in.

"Did you see Nona? I can't believe her." Trina's eyes were wide with disbelief. "She stole my idea. Everything."

"Wait. Slow down a minute." Reno caught Trina around her waist and moved to a terrace window. He pointed to the sky. "That's where you'll be."

Turning her, he caressed her arm, then took her hands. Bringing her closer, he pressed a kiss to her cheek, knowing that would have to suffice for now.

"Reno, what are you doing?" Her voice tickled him and for the briefest second, her body stood evenly with his.

"I was seriously thinking about giving you a congratulatory kiss, but I changed my mind."

Her eyes flashed and in the gray sea, he detected a green speckle of disappointment. "You did?" She laced her fingers with his.

"It's not the right time. We have a contest to win."

She moved just a couple inches away and that was enough for his control to be reinforced. "We?"

"Yes, we. Outside this room, things are going on that you need to be aware of."

"What things?"

"Your ex is here."

"Drake?" Her head snapped back, like she'd taken an elbow to the chin. She took a deep breath. "Why? Is he looking for me?"

Besides her cheeks turning pink, surprisingly, the rest of her remained composed. Reno put his hands in his pockets to keep from touching her again. "He's with Nona," he said carefully. "They're talking to a TV reporter."

Clearly surprised, she parted her lips until full understanding of his words sank in. Her features slid into a well-composed mask.

"Trina—"

"Ms. Crawford, I'm Leeza McIntyre, from WKIT. I'd like to interview you, please."

Reno met the woman's gaze and he wondered how much she'd heard before making her presence known? There was something shady about her and Reno couldn't put his finger on it, but the last thing he was going to do was leave Trina alone with her.

Trina's eyes shifted and she turned.

"I'll be glad to talk to you, Leeza."

"Trina, can I see you for a moment, please?" He was about to take her hand, but she somehow was too close and they ended up with her hands on his ribs.

"I'll be right back," she whispered. "Thank you for being here for me. Don't leave me."

Reno felt the imprint of Trina's hand on his chest for a long time after she went willingly into the lion's den.

Trina felt her anger rising at the question of her upcoming schedule of events. She'd already given an answer two minutes ago. Who was this woman, and why wasn't she paying attention?

"Leeza, as I mentioned, I've booked the High Museum, the Aquarium, Jazz Lights Night Club, Sports Bar at Atlantic Station, and I'm in talks with other companies so that the clients at Suddenlysingleatl.com know they are getting the greatest opportunities to meet other eligible singles."

"All those same venues have been scheduled by Nona Saint. In fact, those plus a few more were booked more than six months ago by Ms. Saint. How do you explain the identical schedule?"

Nona had been part of the Suddenlysingle team and there were few secrets. She'd gone behind Trina's back and double booked.

"I personally booked these events, but as many people don't know, Ms. Saint was an employee of my company. She was privy to much of the information discussed on how to make this opportunity successful."

"Did you use family influence to get bookings at these top-level businesses?"

"No." Trina kept a smile on her face although she wanted to scratch Leeza's eyes out. "I paid the going room rental rate as anyone else would."

Trina stood evenly with Leeza, the tall black woman imposing in her linebackerlike size and height. But Trina wasn't fazed. She'd met tougher women getting a Brazilian wax.

Leeza pressed Nona's schedule into Trina's hand and she let it slip to the floor. No reporter worth her salt would interrupt an interview to retrieve a piece of paper. Leeza looked victorious. "It's the activity plans for your clients."

"Nona and I worked closely since last year until two weeks ago when she walked away with no explanation. I didn't know until seeing her here tonight that she was even in this competition. But it's open to anyone with the money to pay the entry fee."

"She claims Suddenlysingleatl.com was her brainchild."

"I registered the name two years ago."

"Ms. Saint provided a credit card receipt that she in fact paid for the name."

Trina sighed. "Do you have irrefutable proof that I'm now, according to you and Ms. Saint, a liar and a thief? I would caution you and your bosses to think about that question very carefully before you answer. You would not want to make a mistake."

Leeza blinked rapidly.

"It's hard to dispute the facts, Ms. Crawford."

"And it's hard to believe you haven't done your homework before making these ridiculous accusations. But then again, I've never heard of you. Where'd you say you were from?"

"WKIT."

"That's not a station in Florida, Alabama, Tennessee or Mississippi. Where'd you come from, Ms. McIntyre?"

"I'm from Charlotte, North Carolina."

"No, you're not. I personally sent press releases to every news station in North and South Carolina this morning. Have you got a card? I'd like to speak to your station manager."

"Tom, this interview is over." The woman gave the throat-cutting signal to the cameraman who extinguished the light and lowered the camera.

Trina smiled. "You'd better believe it is. When I find out who you really are, you'll be sorry you went to the trouble to deceive me."

"Is that a threat, Ms. Crawford?"

Trina gestured to Tom to roll tape, then waited for him to start. She yanked the microphone from Leeza's hand as the stunned reporter looked on. "Leeza, if I find out that you do not work for WKIT, you will be sorry. That's a wrap."

"Give me that." Leeza tried to snatch the microphone from Trina's hand.

Trina jerked it away, then let it smack Leeza's palm, making her even more angry. "Cut, Tom," Leeza barked.

Reno took Trina by her hand, tugged her to his side, and didn't stop walking. "Let's get your envelope and get out of here so we can do our own celebrating."

"I can't believe them!"

Drake had deceived her and all this time she'd thought they'd parted civilly.

Turning him down on TV had obviously been too much. But why hadn't respecting her wishes been enough to stop him?

Trina hurried inside the room of contestants and endured the endless wait to get her envelope.

She longed to be a Smith, one of her mother's people.

They were uncivilized, uncultured beasts, her mother often said lovingly of her irascible brothers, who, although grown, were known to roll around on the front lawn to settle disputes. Trina had always found them funny. Her mother, however, did not.

Hand-in-hand, Nona and Drake passed within five feet of Trina, and she made a fist, not realizing until Reno folded his hand around hers that he was so close to touching her.

"I want to knock the hell out of them for double-crossing me."

"When we get in the car you can tell me all about it," he whispered and thanked the man who passed Trina her envelope. "Where's the ticket for your coat?" Reno asked as he led her from the crowded room.

She pressed the slip into his palm and a cape of buttery velvet was given to drape over her shoulders. Tears had begun to gather in her eyes and for an instant she and Reno didn't move as they looked at one another. He finally tugged on her clutch bag.

"Don't show them you're upset."

"I wouldn't give them the satisfaction." She hated that her voice wasn't steadier, but she wouldn't cry. "Not even if you hit me in the face with a basketball."

Reno pulled on a sturdy wool coat.

"I apologized for that in college, and you made me carry your books for eight weeks," he said, gathering her close. "Do you know that the chandelier lighting is playing tricks with your earrings?"

"Crystal against crystal."

"Ah," he said, and his eyebrow quirked. "Twelve o'clock, your nemesis and your ex. Shall we give them something to talk about?"

"I'd just be doing it to strike back. I don't want to use you." She looked into his eyes. "But if you—"

"I'm willing to take one for the team." With that he tilted her head back and planted his lips against hers.

Chapter 6

Trina flipped the pages of the extensive menu inside the Waffle House.

Everything about her being there was out of place. Like a princess at a NASCAR race.

"I never knew they had all this food. This is unbelievable." Trina folded the menu and started over.

Reno hadn't been in a Waffle House since his poor college days, but her surprise choice made them being there almost fun. And he wasn't sure of the last time he'd had any fun.

It was well past eleven, the streets far less busy than this morning's rush hour, where he'd been stuck for thirty minutes after picking up prescriptions from the pharmacy.

He was a daylight person, loving how the sun rejuvenated him, made him feel alive and happy. But tonight he'd have happily become nocturnal, if it meant being with Trina.

Even her indecision over selecting a restaurant had been a refreshing change because he and

Dana never agreed on much at the end of their marriage.

Sitting with Trina made him want to whisk her off to Spain to sample paella, or butternut squash soup from South Africa, or chicken tikka masala, an Indian specialty.

"I can't decide." Trina lowered her menu. "What are you thinking?"

"You could have chosen any restaurant in the city. A lot of really nice places are still open. In fact, it's not too late."

"No. I like the menu, and hey, when was the last time I sat on vinyl seats? You can slide right off."

She slumped against the seat, her sexy dress too expensive to look bad. Poised again, she viewed her surroundings and nodded to the men who would later get off to thoughts of her.

"Last chance. We can go to Bacchanalia's or Rathbun's."

"Tell me about the food."

He hesitated. "What food?"

"The best of where you've been."

"I've been around the world," he said, hesitating. "I have too many favorites to list."

"I'm interested, Reno."

Why now? Why hadn't she come to Michigan years ago and said those words to him? He'd have made their relationship work, but the answer came to him as quickly as he knew his name.

Her last name was Crawford. She hadn't needed him.

"Reno, where are you? We're not eating until you talk to me."

He'd longed to have a woman talk to him and

really be interested in what he had to say. "I shouldn't have said around the world. I haven't been to Iceland, but I've been to just about every other major country. I'm going to stop traveling so much later."

"I've traveled, but when I go to France, I shop, so I have no idea what food tastes like." She laughed at herself, her profile sculpted from the genes of queens. "My cousins and I are so superficial, now that I think about it. Now tell me about the food, Reno."

"I had lemon rice and tilapia in Lebanon that was melt-in-your-mouth delicious. Feijoada in Brazil. It's a mixture of black beans, farofa, and pork. Cambulo in Somalia. It's made of adzuki beans. Interestingly enough there aren't any pork dishes in Somalia. Nothing that has died on its own is served, and neither is alcohol."

"Tell me more," she urged softly. Her gaze was focused on his lips. Reno licked them. A tiny smile appeared.

His ego had been plugged with a rocket booster. He'd never been listened to so well. Maybe tonight's kiss had done double duty for her, too.

Witnessing their kiss, Drake and Nona had stopped in their tracks, and he and Trina walked out of the museum as a couple.

"Khado" he continued, "is the most important meal of the day in Somalia, and the biggest. They serve various recipes of rice and vegetables and Soor, which Chloe loves."

"What is it?"

"Cornmeal mashed with sugar, fresh milk, and butter."

"Sounds delicious," Trina said. "You have been just about everywhere. Your favorite food here in America?"

"Hamburgers and fries."

Reno couldn't stop the grin. "What's you favorite pastime, Trina?"

"Shopping. Do you like shopping?" This was a woman's set up question.

"I officially don't like it." Reno kept it real, trying not to laugh.

"You're obviously a sick man," she jokingly looked down her nose at him. "Why not?"

"Shopping is a professional women's sport, and I'm all for women's sports," he sighed, "but you have to have a passion for shopping. For walking hundreds of miles for one pair of shoes when you have seventy others in your closet."

"I beg your pardon. What's wrong with that?"

She gave him the sista-girl head tuck, chin to her chest look.

"Before you pull out your fingernail file and try to stab me, I am a man who enjoys spectator sports. I sit on the couch, look at the stuff you bring home, and say, 'Nice, baby, uh-huh.'"

They both laughed. "That doesn't seem like you." Trina gave up her sista-girl act. "You have to love shopping to some degree. You look very sexy, tonight."

Reno couldn't stop the heat that climbed his body. Sexy? He was ready to strip and wondered if she'd feel the same way.

His face was hot. He wasn't blushing. Men didn't blush.

"I don't know about sexy, but I know there'd have to be major incentives to get me to a mall."

"That could be arranged."

"You say that now, but I suspect I'd be in the mall with no food or water. I'd come home a skeleton with thin lines of eye shadow on the back of my hands that you used as tester. It's not a bright future."

Trina burst out laughing. She reached across the table and patted his hand. "You're funnier than I remember. I like that."

Reno wallowed in the feeling he knew was happiness.

Trina picked up her menu one last time, then put it down. "It's all full of trans fat, so I can pretty much end my life now or enjoy the moment."

"I'd rather enjoy my life," he said, regarding her across the table. "I still can't believe you've lived in Georgia all your life and had never eaten at the Waffle House. How did that happen?"

"You don't know my mother. She's a health nut. I didn't eat McDonald's until I was in the fourth grade and went on a field trip to the Atlanta zoo. But this is very cool, especially after my day."

She spotted the jukebox. "This is the funniest little place I've ever seen! My dad would love this. He's got a ton of records. Don't let him get started dancing to that old school group, The Ojays. The things he and my mother do in the name of dancing are scary. But a real jukebox? I wish I could buy it. I'll call Dad tomorrow and tell him about this."

Reno threw his head back and laughed.

"What?"

"It's like you just materialized from a time warp. Do you want to play a song?" He reached into his pocket for change, but she waved him off.

"I'm too old for that."

Reno had never seen Trina so out of her element, but so comfortable. She was having a good time *and* it was with him. He respected the fact that she wasn't bitter about Drake and Nona's deception.

Her enthusiasm infused him with an energy he only felt during a morning run, joy he didn't want to let go.

"Do you think . . ." she looked around, "it'd be okay if I played a song? Well, they might not like what I choose."

"They select songs everyone loves." Reno gave her all the quarters in his pocket. "Go for it."

All eyes were on Trina as she walked to the jukebox on shoes that glittered like diamonds. Reno took in the whole picture and knew why he'd fallen for her in college and why he'd walked away. The money behind her name reminded him of a casino card with no limit, whereas his money rolled around in a shoebox.

He'd been intimidated by her wealth and had convinced himself that he didn't deserve a woman like her. He'd made her agree to break up, and he'd walked away.

He could honestly say it was one of the biggest regrets of his life.

Trina danced back to the table to "Love Hangover," by Diana Ross. Everybody in the restaurant rocked in their seats.

The tired waitress shuffled by and started moving dirty dishes into the sink. Her blonde-streaked hair was pulled into a tight ponytail, her face sagging with exhaustion. "Short stack, over e, decaf, bac, saus, hash, toast, light, grits."

Trina watched the woman, her mouth open. "What did she just say?"

Reno explained the verbal shorthand. "Pancakes, eggs over easy, decaf coffee, bacon, sausage, hash browns, light toast, and grits."

"Can I help you?" she smiled pleasantly at them.

"How are you tonight, Nancy," Trina asked.

"Tireder than a three-legged hound dog. And I know that ain't a word."

All three laughed. "I'll make it easy on you. I'll have that last order."

"You?" She pointed her pencil at Trina. "Honey, you won't be wearing that dress long if you eat all that."

"This is my first time. I want to try everything. Can you add milk?"

"You betcha. Sir?"

"Coffee for me. I think we'll share."

"Good idea," Trina said.

Nancy rattled off their order. "She's got a great memory."

A man brought his check to the counter and tried to shortchange Nancy. She pulled her pencil from behind her ear and aimed it at him.

"Don't try that mess on me. Here's your change, now get."

The man left with his head down.

"I'm going to remember her. You never know when someone is in need of a career change."

Reno let his gaze rest on Trina. "She's good at her job. Now about tonight—"

"Reno, before we get into the ups and downs, I just want to say thanks for being there for me. I know it sounds funny, but seeing Drake and Nona together was tough. They both betrayed me and stole from me. I can't believe Drake, of all people would do me that way. But now I guess I really know what kind of person he is."

"No problem. After the TV thing, I'd believe anything when it involves him. I think you'll see him again before this is over."

"I really hope not, for his sake."

Reno nodded his thanks to Nancy for the coffee, and poured cream and sugar.

"I feel horrible for rejecting him on TV. It would have been better to accept his proposal, then tell him no after the game. But I felt bullied and disrespected."

Reno was glad she hadn't accepted because he'd have never called. "You two never talked about marriage?"

Trina fingered her crystal earrings that had to have cost over a grand. More than he'd been able to afford as a young man.

"We talked about it, but no was no from the beginning. I'd told Drake no five times that night."

"I guess he couldn't hear you."

"I guess not. Reno, I need to ask you something."

"What is it?"

"What did our kiss mean to you? Were you playing it up for them, or did you really want to kiss me?"

Safe wasn't a place he ventured far from lately; if no meant no, then he needed to do everything possible to turn it around.

"I didn't like that Nona and Drake blindsided you. I thought we should give them something to think about."

"So you didn't enjoy it at all?"

"I didn't say that."

"You're not answering my questions. We've been honest with each other, Reno. Did you really want to kiss me?"

He leaned forward. "There's always been a penalty for being honest with you, Trina."

A startled look crept over her face. "What? Why would you say that?"

"I wanted to kiss you then, and before then, and even now. But what I want most is for you to be my wife and the mother of my two girls. Temporarily. But I can't have that, can I?"

"I already told you—"

He stopped her by placing his hands on hers. "And that's why being honest with you doesn't matter. That kiss doesn't matter, Trina. So let's move on."

The thin glass plates and bowls on the counter seemed less fragile than Trina did right now.

"We're friends, Reno. You can always be honest with me."

Nancy slid Trina's glass of milk on the table. They both sipped.

"Can I make love to you, Trina?"

She seemed to be looking in her glass for the right answer. "That won't solve your problem. It'll create more."

"Now you're not answering my questions."

"What would making love do? Does it get me closer to winning the SBO contest or you closer to getting a wife? No."

"There are intangible benefits, and then tangible." He scooped her leg into his hand. "Relax," he said softly. "Relax."

Caressing from her calf to her ankle, Reno stroked her leg until he felt her muscles release. She sighed and her eyes closed. "Trina?"

"Yes?" She sounded dreamy.

"I'm making love to you right now, and all I can see are tangible benefits."

She pulled her leg away. "I shouldn't have asked that question."

"That's what I'm talking about. Being honest with you is a double edged sword. When you relax, there's this side of you that's damned easy to talk to. You want to know all about me, but I can't penetrate that outer core of Trina Crawford without hitting a brick wall."

"You want a relationship, Reno."

"What's wrong with that?"

"I can't be in one right now. I'm trying to get my company off the ground, win a contest, and recover from a breakup," she said, much softer.

"Fine, I understand."

Her brows arched at the ends. "You're lying."

"I've never had to *persuade* a woman to marry me or sleep with me. I won't now."

Shock and rejection split her features. He didn't want to hurt her, but talking like this hurt him.

Nancy delivered plates full of food, dropped thin napkins and left.

"Thank you," Trina said as she lined her lap with napkins, then started eating. "Can we talk about the company for a few minutes?"

"We're always safe talking about business. Shoot."

"I decided to keep to my schedule. I won't change just because Nona and I have some of the same venues scheduled. She did that to sabotage me."

"This is the perfect opportunity to prove you have better ideas than her. Keeping the same schedule and marketing to the same audience is only going to bring minimal, if any, success."

"I booked these facilities." He saw the stubborn streak he'd had to deal with in college. "If the event doesn't happen, I won't get my deposit back. Besides, I don't want her to think she's got me on the run. I didn't steal anything from her."

"The public won't care. If people were just at the High Museum, they won't go back two nights later to the same type of event."

"You have toast on your face."

Reno swiped at his cheek. "Did I get it?"

"No." Trina chewed her eggs. She wiped her own mouth and tapped beside her lip. "Right here."

He tried again. Finally she leaned over and wiped his mouth. Her gaze remained fixed on

his lips. Reno wanted to take her someplace trop-
ical and make love to her until the middle of the
afternoon.

Fighting his attraction to her wouldn't be easy,
and she wasn't making it easier by giving off
mixed signals.

At Georgia State, she hadn't been shy about
showing her attraction.

They'd both been on basketball teams, and
once the women finished practicing, Trina
would come to the men's gym and get chased
out by the coach for trying to practice with the
guys. But she kept coming back until the coach
begrudgingly let her practice.

She got knocked down, fouled, stepped on, and
harassed for being the only "Barbie" in a room full
of men.

But she hadn't backed down. She'd fought
back, and soon the guys began to respect her
and teach her.

Reno would leave the gym at the last whistle,
but after showering, he'd head to the top of the
bleachers. From up there he didn't have to hide
his admiration or the mad crush he had on her.

She was always trying to dunk the ball and
missing. The first game of the season, she'd
shocked everyone and cleared the rim by an
inch. But every attempt after that had failed.

One day she'd been trying for three hours and
kept getting stuck on the front of the rim.

Reno forced himself up on tired legs, his ath-
letic pants swishing in the heat of the afternoon.
Trina had turned at his footfalls. His knees had

been stiff, and his back hurt too, but he'd seen what he was looking for, what he felt inside.

Drive and desire.

He'd pounded the ball from her hands and told her if she wanted to dunk, she'd have to get mad enough to take it.

He'd run with the ball, leapt in the air, creating a circle with his right hand palming the ball, and then slammed it down the rim.

Reno hadn't even bothered to bounce the ball back to her. Instead he'd taunted her.

He'd told her pretty girls like her wouldn't get what they wanted out of life because they wouldn't ever learn how to work hard.

He'd left after that and hadn't spoken to her again for two weeks. He had to run her off, or else he'd flunk out of school for being in love with her.

She'd kept coming back and he watched from a distance. Every day she practiced hour after hour, but she still couldn't dunk.

She was frustrated, and she'd throw the ball at the board and yell her head off.

From up high in the bleachers, he could admire her without getting teased, and he knew that she was almost there.

The last game of the season was UGA against the Tennessee Lady Volunteers, and speculation had been high about whether Trina would even try a dunk.

She'd focused on the game with an intensity he'd never seen before. The Tennessee team was the best, and Trina had an advantage. She couldn't stand them.

The game had been tight, down to the last twelve seconds and Trina, who'd been matched against their center, got elbowed in the mouth. She'd bled, and the Vols had called for her to be seen by the doctor.

A trip to the locker room would end her season. Georgia was down by one. Reno had stood with the rest of the men's team, waiting anxiously. Trina sat for twenty seconds. She wiped her bloody mouth, put her teeth guard in, and when she stood up, he knew she wasn't leaving.

She took her position on the foul line, shot the ball and it bounced and rolled off the rim. The ref bounced the ball back to her and she shot high, and he'd wondered what she was thinking, when it bounced against the back of the rim and popped out.

Tennessee moved the ball to half court when the guard for Georgia had stripped it from the guard and lobbed it high for Trina. Reno could see the determination on her face and when she jumped, he watched her body fly. When she caught the ball, there was only one inevitable conclusion. She had slammed it home.

The crowd had gone crazy, but Reno watched her to the end as she looked at her hands clutching the rim, and the Lady Vols center beneath her legs.

She'd let go and landed on the floor and the buzzer sounded.

That night, she'd been on top of the world.

All season he'd avoided her, not letting the fire inside of him direct his emotions. But he'd seen in Trina another fire. One that matched his. Drive and determination.

Long after the gym had been locked, Reno had gone looking for Trina, and heard that she was looking for him, but he'd missed seeing her at every party. Finally he found himself outside her dorm, looking up at the window. Her light was still on.

Nervous, he'd been unsure whether to walk up to her third-floor room, or go to his dorm and ease his own frustration.

An invisible pull propelled his feet forward and when a freshman had exited the door and held it for him, Reno had taken it as a good sign.

He'd knocked gently, wondering if she was already in bed.

Just when he'd thought she wouldn't answer, Trina had opened the door and her long hair was down for the first time, accentuating her exquisite beauty. He'd pulled the top from the box he'd been carrying for three hours and had shown it to her.

A slow smile had spread across her face and she'd invited him in. They'd been a couple until he'd transferred.

Now, here he sat across from her in the Waffle House as if eight years hadn't slipped by.

"You went somewhere," she said. "You used to do that, and I would wonder what was so interesting in your head."

The memory faded. "Remembering the old days."

"Care to share?" she asked, eating her grits.

"No, it's . . . nothing. Would you like something else?"

"No, but I'd like to hear any new thoughts on my company. What do you think I should do?"

"I suggest you scrap your entire plan and start from ground zero."

"Do you know how much I've spent on the website, flyers, e-mails? I can't walk away. I'm not going to be intimidated by them, Reno. You should know me better than that."

"There was a man named Elisha Gray who applied for a caveat to patent the phone in 1876. Hours after Alexander Graham Bell."

"Don't get bookish on me, Mr. Merriwether. I just don't think I have to go to all that trouble. People who know me know I wouldn't steal anything. Crawfords don't steal."

"Have your clients do something worthwhile. Don't charge them for facilitating."

"I'll have to think about the first part, but I'm nonnegotiable on the second," Trina said. "I already advertised that we charge."

"Okay, but not for community events."

"Agreed," she said, finishing her milk.

"Have you collected any fees in advance for any other of your events?"

"No."

"Next time do an online pay company. Once they pay the ten-dollar fee, they're more likely to come. Do you really think you're going to have a record turnout?"

"Why shouldn't I? My cocktail party/happy hour on Friday will prove that I'm about quality.

People aren't going to be suckered by a few cheap gifts and a fake smile."

Yeah they would. They'd been suckered by less.

"Pass the syrup," he said, and poured a good helping on his pancakes.

"You're going to get sick," Trina said, finishing her third piece of bacon.

"We can share the same cardiologist," he said dryly.

"Ha-ha. I'm as healthy as a horse."

"Said the woman who just devoured sausage and bacon in the same sitting."

"Be quiet, know-it-all."

Trina eyed the last piece of bacon speculatively.

"Go ahead. You won't feel good about yourself if you don't."

"You don't know everything, Reno," she said and chewed. "I'm eating it because I don't want to insult Nancy. And I already made a pact with God not to eat any more pork after Memorial Day."

"Good luck. You're stronger than I am. I still want to partner with you, Trina. I have a lot to offer. I've already been there."

She shook her head. "I appreciate it, but doing this solo—with a little advice on the side— is best for me."

Reno tried not to let the blow to his self-confidence show. "I know what's it's like to start a business, but you do your thing. Do me a favor, though."

"What is it?"

"You're going to have to modify your original

paperwork by removing Nona's name. Add mine as a just-in-case. You'll have to do it tomorrow before you open your envelope. Just be sure to take the envelope with you to show it's still sealed. Adding me means nothing, but you can't add on to your staff after the envelope is opened. Nona probably didn't think to add Drake."

Trina shrugged. "He's pretty clever. I didn't even know he was attracted to Nona."

"Good. From now on, we refer to them as the competitor. You're the winner. Psych yourself up."

Trina leaned in, stirring her milk. "Thank you for understanding, Reno." Silence hung between them as she sipped her drink. "How's the hunt going for you?"

"I'm still looking, but optimistic."

Reno wouldn't look at her, because then she might see how much he wanted her help. He needed her, but he'd have to proceed slowly if he was to going to try to get what he wanted.

He ate the last of his pancakes.

"You're a handsome man. Someone will turn up."

"I'm very close to bribing a woman at this point."

"Oh, Reno. I'm sorry."

"Don't be. You have an agenda, and . . ." his words drifted off as his guilt increased. He planned to have her. He just didn't know how. "I'll find what I need soon enough. A friend of a friend knows someone who needs a visa to stay in the U.S. She's a resident at Atlanta Memorial, but she's going to have to leave in a couple months. We may be able to work something out."

Besides looking apprehensive, Trina didn't seem as if she were going to change her mind.

"That sounds shady."

"I need a woman so I don't mind if she needs me. Can we talk about something else?"

Trina swallowed. "Sure. Sorry."

"Things will work out for the best. No worries. Do you want dessert?"

"If I eat another bite, I'll explode. Little bits of Trina splattered all over the walls. That won't be cute."

"Lucky walls," he said, and a blush raced up her neck to her cheeks. Reno could picture her the way a man in love saw his wife.

The assessment startled him. He couldn't act on his feelings of love, so he'd have to find someone else quickly.

"Still hungry?" Nancy asked pleasantly.

Reno scanned the table and Trina did the same. Empty white plates covered the surface.

"I think we're good, Ms. Nancy." Trina dropped her last napkin on the table.

"You are a darlin'," the woman said. "What's your name?"

"Trina Crawford."

"Ms. Trina, I have my own catering business and if you ever need anything, I'd be glad to make it for you. I know I don't look like much in this pretty little frock, but I clean up real good, and I cook even better."

"I'm going to be calling you, Ms. Nancy."

"Hey, call me Nancy."

"I'm Trina. Here's my card. I'll write your number on this one for me to keep."

They exchanged numbers and hugs. Nancy patted Reno's shoulder. "Be good to her. I'd better go. See that bus full of boys that just pulled in? They won't feed themselves."

A baseball team exited the chartered bus.

Trina reached for her purse. "I'm going to call her. Breakfast tonight is my treat."

"Okay."

"Reno, you keep surprising me. I didn't expect that."

"I'm unpredictable, so you'd better watch out."

She extended her hand and he helped her up. Trina paid the check and they headed to the door.

Nancy snapped up the money on her way to another table, looked at the thirty-dollar tip and waved as they left.

The team stood to the side as Trina walked out. A chorus of "Ma'ams" followed her.

The cold February air had dipped into the twenties and Trina shivered as Reno opened the car door.

She slid inside and waited for him.

"That's a cute car seat. Where'd you get that cushion?"

"My cousin in Virginia. She makes all of her kid's clothes. They've got terrible allergies."

Trina fumbled with the seat belt in the Lexus. "Have you got it?"

"Yes. It's just stuck."

"Nancy said you were going to get fat. You didn't believe her."

Trina laughed and rounded her hands as if she were going to choke him. "Keep it up, funny man. You'll end up sleeping in the parking lot."

He turned on the car. "Let me help you or we might not leave."

Trina glanced at him, then at the seat belt. "Okay, if I must. But no—"

Before she could finish, Reno's lips molded to hers, pressing, then retreating until she opened for him. His tongue slid against her lips and she nipped at it, welcoming it into her mouth. She tasted good, and being this close to her made him want her more. His hand was nearly at her breast when he caressed her side; then he pulled the belt and snapped it into the buckle.

Her eyes were still closed as he drove through the quiet streets of Atlanta. She wasn't sleeping, but she wasn't speaking either. He didn't regret the kiss, only his timing.

He'd taken advantage of her.

Just like Drake, he hadn't respected her wishes.

Reno turned into the dark parking lot of the museum and pulled alongside her car.

"Thank you." Trina unfastened her seat belt and Reno captured her hand.

"I shouldn't have kissed you. I'm sorry if I made you uncomfortable."

She turned to get out. "I can't explain why I have feelings for you when I thought I had feelings for Drake two weeks ago. I just can't touch you because . . . the attraction is there, Reno. But I need time to sort things out."

"Sort what out? You're not with him anymore. You're giving him so much of you when you should be thinking of yourself and someone that genuinely wants you."

"That's not fair," she said. "If I didn't take this time now, I could stumble and fall."

"What's wrong with falling, if there's someone who wants to catch you? Don't answer that. You do what you have to do. I won't make another move until you want me to. I promise."

Trina looked so hurt. Tonight her emotions had criss-crossed the spectrum, and all he wanted to do was take her in his arms and hold her. But he would leave her alone if it killed him.

"Are you coming to the High Museum to the launch reception?"

"I've got another commitment on Friday. Let's catch up next week."

"You have to be there. I want you there, Reno."

He needed to focus all his attention on finding a wife, and hanging around Trina wouldn't help him. He had to tell her no. "I need to focus all my attention on finding a wife, Trina."

She exhaled twice. "Don't run from our friendship."

He bit his tongue, tart saliva warning him of the blood beneath the surface.

He wanted to ask the same of her, but didn't. "I'll see what I can do."

Her smile sank into him like sustenance to an empty stomach. "I'll look for you. See you Friday night at the High."

Chapter 7

Trina knew a sinking ship when she saw one, and this event was her *Titanic*.

Tracey and Trisha milled about in the signature colors of Suddenlysingleatl.com—feminine pink and black—passing out little handbags and asking the women to carry them to work for the next thirty days.

When the bags had arrived at the office this morning, Trina had been baffled. She hadn't ordered them, and just as she was getting ready to decline the shipment, Reno had called, asking if she'd received his marketing gift. He explained his strategy in sixty seconds. The bags were to be given to women who'd paid the registration fee. They'd carry the cute totes, and other women would ask about them.

Word of mouth. She had to admit, the idea was brilliant.

Trina had signed for the bags, but when she found out they'd been paid for, she'd written out a check to deliver to Reno tonight. She couldn't take donations over the limit of five hundred dollars, and Reno had made sure they were compliant.

A few women who carried the bags through the museum looked cute, but the event itself was a flop. Only fifty people had shown up, and it was a Friday night. She'd invited more than fifteen hundred. Reno had been right. She and Nona were working from the same customer base, and since Nona had her launch here last night, it looked as if Trina was copying.

Nona's event had been free, and she'd given out collector's watches. Trina shook her head. Reno had been right on every point.

Disgusted, Trina got up from behind the greeting table and called Trisha over. "Can you sit in for me? I need to stretch my legs."

"Sure."

"You shouldn't have let Reno get away. Now he's got somebody and she's beautiful. Over your shoulder, to the right." Trisha picked up the envelope and turned around to look casual as she spied. Goodness, she was gorgeous.

She wondered if this was the doctor he'd mentioned.

Jealousy spun through her, and for an unlikely reason. She wanted Reno to chase her, but it looked as if he'd found a new pair of stilettos to admire.

The woman saw Trina and stared her down, just as Reno turned and saw her.

Trina stuck her leg through the thigh-high split. "Reno," she said, sounding more Southern than she intended. "Introduce me to your guest."

His gaze took a leisurely stroll up her Ralph

Lauren dress. Finally he met her gaze. "Um. Hmm." He chuckled. "This is embarrassing."

The woman's look was scathing. "*Dr.* Isabelle Fisher. I don't shake hands. Germs."

"You're the physician Reno told me about. Nice to meet you." Trina moved the offending hand back to her side. "Of course. I wouldn't want to give you *E. coli.*"

The woman's eyes widened. "You have it?"

Trina wiggled her fingers. "One never knows."

"You're right. That's why no man touches me without going through a battery of tests."

Even Reno looked shocked.

"What's your specialty?" Trina asked, being polite when she wanted to cough on Dr. Fisher and watch her run.

"Cosmetic surgery."

Somehow, she wasn't surprised. Trina smiled graciously. "Why don't you two go ahead through the museum, and I'll see you a bit later?"

Isabelle looked Brazilian and black, but Trina wasn't sure with a last name of Fisher. The doc was gorgeous, but the parts of her that had been enhanced were so obvious that she looked like a doll that had been glued back together. Why was Reno giving her the time of day? She was all wrong for him.

"Of course," Reno said, his hand lightly on Isabelle's back as she moved a few steps away.

"Reno, I want to talk about the terms of the agreement," Trina heard Isabelle say as they walked off. "We haven't talked about payment."

"We can talk about that later, Isabelle. We're here to have a good time."

Regret and the knowledge that she couldn't do what he wanted filled Trina with guilt.

She made her way to a table, greeting clients. A small line had formed. Unfortunately, it was over too quickly, leaving her with free time on her hands.

She grabbed a handful of totes and strolled through the museum, offering them to women who promised to get a friend to sign up. Twice, she went back to the table, each time glancing around. She knew she was looking for Reno.

"May I have a bag, please?"

Isabelle was at the table without Reno.

Trina handed her one. "How are you enjoying your evening?"

"I'm bored and that's not a good sign. Reno is talking to a male nurse. What a waste of school. Why not go ahead and become a doctor?" Isabelle glared as she assessed Trina without shame.

"Reno said you were friends from college. Does he bore you with talk about his daughter?"

"You are familiar with his situation," Trina said, stunned. "I got the impression you were going to get something out of it, too."

"I was. But to give up all those months of my life for a middle-class lifestyle, I can do better." She looked around as if her business was done. "Can you tell him I didn't feel well?" she asked, her poofy lips looking so steroid-enhanced she could have bounded home.

Trina couldn't believe the woman's nerve. So what that she was a doctor? "Reno's your date. You tell him."

Isabelle regarded Trina with a look of superiority.

"When Reno told me we were going to an event to support a female friend, I told him it wasn't going to work because women are generally jealous of me."

"You don't have anything I want," Trina informed her. "I won't ever be jealous of you or anyone."

"Female friend," she laughed sarcastically. "If I wanted him, I'd have him. It's clear to me you don't know your place."

Without a backwards glance at Reno, Isabelle marched out the door. She walked down the breezeway to the street where a stretch limo picked her up.

What the hell, Trina thought. She turned and saw Reno coming toward her, his stride confident. Trina came around the table and headed him off.

"According to *your woman, I don't know my place.* Is that witch crazy? Does she know who she's talking to? Where'd you find her? I know you can do better than that. Because if you can't, I—"

Trina didn't realize that she'd grabbed Reno's arm until he pointed to her fingers digging into his muscle. "You'll what?" he asked.

Trina loosened her grip. "I'm sorry. You okay?"

"Nothing a tetanus shot won't fix."

"Don't get it from the black widow."

"You'll what, Trina?" he said casually, while stepping out of the way for a passing waiter. As much as she tried not to touch him, their bodies brushed and she was confused again.

"Nothing."

"We're back to being a great conversationalist. My arm, please?"

She'd dug her nails in again. "Oh, come on. You're being such a girl." Trina guided him away from the view of the street toward the gift shop.

Remembering his aversion to shopping, she headed for the buffet.

"I used to tell you that."

"All the time—when you were speaking to me."

"Come on, Ms. Great Memory. Let's go on a tour."

The High had the most unique design with beautiful white wrapping ramps going up into the museum. Each level boasted different exhibits, and with the sparse crowd, the higher they went, the less people they encountered.

They reached the top and the music from below dusted their ankles with soft melodies.

"How would you say things are going tonight?" he asked, walking off a bit.

"I paid twenty-five hundred dollars to rent this place and for the band. Fiscally, it's a failure."

He nodded, looking down at the thin groups of people. "I was here last night."

"You were? How could you?"

"You needed a spy, didn't you? Or did you send a gray-eyed Crawford?"

Trina reached up to rub his back in thanks, then dropped her hand. "You're right again. I'm sorry. All I seem to do is apologize."

"We shouldn't stop."

"Why?" her voice was now a whisper. The music had stopped and voices carried up like poetry.

"You might run over my foot with your car," he said, moving close to her.

A giggle burst out of her. "There are exceptions, but for ordinary things like me telling you you'd be making the mistake of a lifetime by thinking of Isabelle past tonight, well, I would apologize, if I thought you'd forgive me."

Reno reached for her.

She felt him bringing her closer and closer until their bodies connected like a key in a lock.

"What are you doing?" she whispered, completely engulfed by him.

"Dancing with you," he said, and they began to sway to the music of silence.

Then the band began right on tempo as if Reno were the maestro.

Trina let all of her rules, defenses, and her fears leave her body as she danced with a man who was the perfect partner.

She was scared. She wanted Reno, but the package he came with frightened her, and she wasn't talking about the girls.

The music ended too soon and as if she were awakened from a dream, Trina tried to slip from his arms, but he wouldn't let her go.

"First thoughts," he said and she remembered those were the first words he'd said to her when he'd come into her room the night of her game.

She said them again. "I want you here."

"Are you positive?"

"Yes. I don't want you to marry her. She's not right for you. Let me help you."

Reno ran his hand up to her neck. "Those are the magic words, but I don't believe that sweet mouth is saying what I want to hear. So, baby, how can you help me?"

"I can find someone better than Isabelle."

"Better than you? You know it's you that I want."

Trina's heartbeat raced. "Better than me. There's someone way better than me. I'll find her. Just not Gazelle."

He laughed. "Isabelle."

"I know."

His fingers laced with Trina's. "Speaking of . . . I'd better get back. She'll wonder what happened to me."

"You'll have to retest for germs."

"You're cute," he said, jokingly sarcastic.

Trina snagged his hand, slowing their descent. "She left."

Reno stopped on the main level and brought Trina around to face him. "I figured as much when I didn't hear her screeching because you were with me."

"You okay?" she asked, enjoying their public intimacy because she knew this was as far as she could go.

"Better than okay."

He looped his arms with hers and walked through the common area. "Want to know what I learned from Nona's camp?"

"I'd love to."

"Similar set up with the band. She gave out very nice watches." Reno dug in his pocket and handed Trina the pocket timepiece. It was exquisite. A diamond commanded the twelve and six o'clock hours while tapered hands represented the hours and minutes. Encased in black and gold, the timepiece had a classic look. Not unlike other watches she'd seen, but certainly not something she'd expect as a gift for this type of event. Nona was taking this very seriously. The back was numbered and signed. A signature piece.

"She's going all out. I wonder if she exceeded the five-hundred limit?"

"Definitely, but do you want to pursue a challenge against her to the committee?"

"No," Trina said, considering the ramifications. "She'll bitch about everything and the publicity wouldn't be worth it. If the committee finds out, it won't be because of me."

"I like that about you."

Trina couldn't look him in the eye. Why couldn't Reno just want to hang out with her? They would be very happy.

"Nona had wristbands, and she handed out cards to the people who were members, asking them to join."

"We did that on check-in. They have to join to come in."

"What's your price to join?"

"Nineteen ninety-nine."

"Good, hers is thirty dollars."

"How's that good? She's making more."

"People weren't joining. She sold food and drinks."

"Ours is free." Trina looked at the table. "Nobody's eating it, but that's neither here nor there. And we had open bar for two hours."

They walked over to the registration table. Trina checked the computer and then handed out forms to her cousins. "These need to be completed and collected. Can you take care of it for me?"

The girls moved into action, and Trina returned to Reno's side. She wanted to be with him more than anyone she'd met this evening. There were some handsome men here, professional men who were usually her type.

But after Reno arrived, she found she couldn't remember the name of a single man she'd met. What a relief they had name tags.

Trina greeted guests and introduced Reno to women as they passed. She checked on him occasionally to see if he was having fun, but when he looked at her she just wanted to rescue him.

His expression said he was so far from fun they weren't even in the same time zone.

Trina sent a stream of women his way, but none stuck, and finally she stopped mingling and went to him. Reno seemed unable to walk without holding her hand so she let him.

"Was there anything else I should know?"

"We definitely need to retool your approach," Reno said, handing the watch to Trina. "She's having her next event at the Aquarium. The day before yours."

Trina held her stomach because she felt sick. "Okay. We can't have another event like this. I lost a ton of money on catering that didn't get eaten and a building that wasn't full."

"Can we meet tomorrow, my house?"

"Your place?" she asked.

"My nanny has a doctor's appointment, so I have Chloe."

Trina couldn't think of a reason not to join

him except the idea of meeting his little girl again made her heart race. Which was completely irrational.

First, she had tons of female cousins, and second, women didn't intimidate her. But the child was four and her father wanted to marry Trina. For some reason, Trina wasn't running for the hills every time Reno was near. She needed him, too, and he was willing to help.

Reno was waiting for an answer.

"Sure, I can come by," Trina heard herself saying. "Where do you live?"

He gave her directions and they continued to stroll and greet the guests.

Women eyed Reno as if he were filet mignon. They approached, offering him their numbers.

He graciously shook their hands and explained that he was with someone. They eyed Trina, knew she was the company owner, and moved on.

Tracey gave Trina a computer tablet to sign. She pointed out a few things and Trina nodded. Then Tracey looked at Reno. "The lady you were with returned about five minutes ago."

"Why?"

"She said she'd have a better chance with you, but you were apparently holding hands with Trina, and she got pissed."

Trina pulled her lips inside her mouth for a few seconds. "She's gone?"

"She said she considers what you did cheating. Anyway, she met another man, made a phone call, and they headed for the parking lot. Want me to go explain?"

Trina waited for Reno.

"No thanks, Tracey. This is all your fault. Don't try that innocent act on me."

"I didn't do anything," she said, trying not to laugh.

"Of course not." Reno said as he smiled.

Soon, they were all laughing.

"I saved you from a life of hell." Though the teasing words were from her heart, Tracey hadn't helped his situation any.

"She wasn't that bad."

"Reno, I made you a promise and I intend to keep it."

"If you can't?" he said, confronting Trina in front of her family.

"Of course I can. We're aiming to have the largest database of single women in the state. There's a woman out there."

"I shouldn't have hogged your time."

Reno shrugged. "I suspect Isabelle wouldn't have passed the final test anyway."

"What's that?"

"Chloe."

"What about her?" Trina wasn't sure why she would have a problem with a little kid.

Tracey walked by and handed them two glasses of white wine. Reno sipped. "She has to like whoever I choose or the deal is off."

Trina accepted a plate of shrimp from her sister. She and Reno shared shrimp and cocktail sauce while the band began playing "Sweetest Taboo" by Sade.

"She's how old? Four? What does she know about liking people?"

"She has a personality. If she doesn't like the

woman, I don't want either to suffer. Chloe's already sad."

"Well, why expose her to the woman at all?"

"The judge in the court proceedings wants to see us as a family. If something rings false, then we don't get Christina."

"You already know her name?" she said softly.

The sweetness endeared her. She felt herself weakening. He already loved the child he'd never met.

"They told me it was Christina. She's still at the orphanage and I've got only a month left. Isabelle wasn't perfect, but her stipulations weren't too bad. If Christina is anything like her sister, well—I can't handle them both."

"Of course you can."

"Look, do you mind if we talk about something else? What are you going to do with all this food?" Reno walked along the table of food and Trina trailed him. She'd chosen a New Orleans theme with gumbo, crawfish, crab-stuffed mushrooms, corn casserole, fresh shrimp, hush puppies, dirty rice, oyster dressing, and jambalaya. Most of it had gotten cold, but it was still good and there was still a lot of it.

"Eat more food," she urged him. "If I think too hard about the money I lost, the vein in my neck might burst."

"That vein only comes out when you're overexerted. Or it used to."

"You have an unbelievable memory. I wish I could give this food away."

"Why can't you?"

"I guess I could. I know there's a women's shelter not too far from here."

"There is? I only know about the men's shelter off Luckie Street." Reno guided her to an unoccupied couch where they rested with plates of food.

"The location of the women's shelter is a secret. I'll make a phone call and see if they can take delivery at this time of night."

"Ok," Reno said. "The men's shelter isn't a secret. I only have my car, but we can pack as much food in there as you want and I'll drive it over. Dr. Kendu Rogers is an old friend."

Her smile was grateful. "Reno, you don't have to do that. It's been a long night and I was responsible for your date running off."

"No, you weren't. My date believes in kismet."

"Fate?" she said, waving good night to clients that walked by.

He nodded. "The man she left with could have just walked in the door, and if she believed he was supposed to be hers, she would have left with him."

"She sounds like a nut, if you ask me." Trina was relieved that Reno laughed. "I apologize. My mouth is terrible tonight. I appreciate you coming here and everything you've done, I wish I could repay you."

He offered her a hand up.

"We're going to wind things down a bit," Deion, Trina's brother, said into the microphone, his dreads and pretty gray eyes making some women swoon. "So find someone beautiful and wrap your arms around them. If you haven't made a love connection, join Suddenlysingleatl.com, and tell your friends. We're System."

"You can start by dancing with me." Reno kept her at a respectful distance and Trina moved a little closer. They'd been friends and lovers in the past. Both knew why she couldn't get involved with him.

"I want everything to work out with Chloe."

"I do, too."

She leaned into Reno and he accepted her. "The night of the event, I put my schedule on the website, and I checked Nona's. Mine is different because . . . I took your advice."

She leaned away, just enough to see his face. He didn't look smug or superior. Reno looked happy for her.

Was this love? This comfortable, safe feeling of having a man who was affectionate and kind in her arms? Trina wasn't sure. Nothing she'd had before felt like this.

Like a magnet to metal, he held her close again. "What advice?"

"I'm going to have my clients do something worthwhile. I made a deal with Crawford Construction to help build a house. The program is called Next Step and they build homes for low income families."

"Sounds altruistic. Be sure to get the necessary health releases from everyone."

"I know, Reno. I love the idea of men and women working together in the community. We can mix and match everybody until the house is done. We'll be making dreams come true for people who need help. It'll be very successful."

When Reno hugged her this time, everything

around them stopped and she held on to the feeling, wanting to seal it in her memory.

Slowly the music started again and they just swayed.

"That's what I'm talking about. It's thoughtful and helpful. So the rest of the schedule is—"

"Scrapped."

She laughed against his shoulder. "Go ahead and say I told you so."

Reno leaned back and said, "I told you so."

"You're the only person I've told," she said to him. "I'm a little paranoid—"

"Your secrets are always safe with me," Reno said. "What time are you coming by tomorrow?"

"Ten or eleven."

"Good," Reno said. "Don't look now but you have company."

Trina turned around, and the newscaster and cameraman for Fox 5 News were at the registration desk. She walked over, Reno trailing at a distance. "Brett, welcome to Suddenlysingleatl.com's first event."

Brett's eyes sparkled.

"Wow, you know me," he gushed, in that silly way of his that made people feel comfortable. "Trina, I have a message for you from the Small Business Corporation, sponsors of the small business contest. Can we take the stage for a moment?"

Trina nodded and hurried over to the band, and they stopped playing.

She waved Brett over. "We don't have a stage, but you certainly have our attention. Everyone, this is Brett from Fox 5 News. Please welcome him and his cameraman," she leaned toward him, "I'm sorry, what's your name?"

He looked unaccustomed to attention as he lifted the camera from his eye. "Uh, Warren."

"Please welcome Brett and Warren."

Applause greeted the two men.

"Trina, would you like to know why I'm here?" Brett said, "Do you like surprises?"

Reno knew that was a no, but Trina was handling her business. She folded her hands in front of her. Reno didn't laugh. "Brett, I love surprises."

All of the people who knew Trina cracked up. She didn't acknowledge them, but played to the crowd by blinking and looking sweet at the same time.

"I think some people would disagree, but I'll have to ask them later. Are you ready for what I've got?"

"I don't have to eat a bug, do I?"

Brett withdrew an envelope from his pocket, enjoying her humor. "No. So far, they haven't given me any challenges like that. Just questions. I've got one that has to be verified with your computer that is linked with the SBC contest computer. If you are correct, you get the prize in this envelope. If not, you've got me for the rest of the night eating from the lovely buffet."

Trina nodded to Tracey to bring in the computer as the crowd laughed.

"Are you ready, Trina?" Brett asked with much fanfare, the crowd cheering. "Come on guys, help her," he said to the audience.

"Yes. I'm ready. What's my question?"

"As of ten o'clock, how many new singles had joined your organization? You've got ten seconds."

"Since ten o'clock tonight or this morning?"

"Good question," Brett grinned, looking smitten. He was eating out of her hand. "Tonight," Brett said.

"As of tonight at ten we had thirty-eight people who joined."

"Is that your final answer," he said, dropping his voice to ask the popular game show question.

"Yes," she said confidently. "That's my final answer."

Brett pulled out a computerized data card and inserted it into the official computer.

"We will know in just a second if this lovely lady is correct, and then maybe someone can teach this boy with two left feet how to do the electric slide."

The audience cheered again for Brett, who did a strange dance sideways.

Trina looked at the computer, but didn't touch it.

A bell sounded and the card popped out, which Brett pocketed. He then held the computer away from everyone's eyes. "Is Trina right?" he asked the crowd.

She got a robust round of applause, and Brett turned the laptop around for everyone to see. "You're correct!"

Trina's arms shot into the air and joy lit her face.

Reno saw her coming for him. He opened his arms and she jumped in.

"We did it," she breathed against his cheek.

Before he could speak, she had gone back to Brett and her very happy clients.

"This is what you've earned. Trina, would you do me the honor of holding the microphone for me while I open the envelope? You do want to know what you've won, right?"

"Yes, I do, Brett," she said, excitement making her move. The band began to softly play an upbeat tune.

Brett moved his shoulders. Despite what he said, he had some soul in him.

"Trina, I believe you'll like this. You've won four hundred new enrollees into Suddenlysingle-atl.com. These clients came from a database that is now out of business, so you are the happy recipient of more single clients. Hopefully you can help them make a romantic connection."

Applause ripped through the crowd and Trina's excitement was catchy. She hugged Brett with one arm, and Reno admired her sensitivity to the shorter man. She didn't bear hug him and give him a face full of breast, although the idea of her breasts did things to his mind and body. He sighed. She needed time and he didn't have any. Reno hated that his brain refused to accept that.

His cell phone rang and he stepped into the corner to take the call. "Hello?"

"Mr. Merriwether?"

"Yes?"

"This is Amiah from Exclusive Love Connection. Is this a good time?"

"Yes, what can I do for you?"

"Good news. We have three women that match

your profile exactly. We'd like to set up appointments for tomorrow."

Trina spotted Reno and he waved at her. "That's great."

"Is ten in our office good for you?"

"I can't. My nanny has a commitment tomorrow and I'll have my daughter. Can they come to my house? I have an office and a staff member can be present if that would make you comfortable."

"Sir, we understand you operate your business out of your home. I think having a staff member present is a great idea. The meetings will be scheduled on the hour. I'll let the ladies know you'll start at ten. I'll e-mail you a confirmation. Goodnight."

"Thanks, Amiah. Goodnight."

Trina's eyes held questions. Reno took her hands and led her to the dance floor.

"I've hired several agencies to help me find a wife. One of them just called and said they have three women that might be a good match."

"Three? Wow." Her expression was unreadable. "You look happy."

Reno glanced down at her. "It gets me closer to getting what I want. What everybody wants."

"What's that?"

"What you have, Trina. A loving family."

Chapter 8

Reno straightened Chloe's dress for the third time and wished she'd get off his lap. Ever since she'd gotten up she'd been his new twenty-four-pound appendage.

"Miss, little girl." He tapped her on the shoulder until she swung around and looked at him.

"You have to get down or you're going with Mrs. Teralyn. I have a meeting in five minutes." He held up his watch. "That's when the big hand is here and moves to here. Now, can I please have my lap back so I can get some work done?"

Chloe bumped her head hard against his chest again and again. She was angry, and his patience was quickly evaporating with the bright morning sun.

Finally Reno couldn't take it. He picked her up, put her on the floor and went back to his desk.

Before he could sit, she'd grabbed the back of his pants and sunk her teeth into his leg.

Reno yanked his daughter up by her frilly

dress until they were nose to nose. "Have you lost your mind?"

She didn't move.

"Answer me. Did you bite me?"

She nodded and two big tears spilled over her eyelids.

"Chloe Lydia Merriwether, no crying. You're in big trouble. Do I ever bite you?"

She shook her head no.

"Do I ever bump you?"

She shook her head again and two more tears fell, and she hiccupped to stop from crying.

"You don't talk, so I don't know what's going on in your head. But you will not hit and you will not bite. Understood?"

She nodded.

"You're in a time out, little girl. Go lay down in your wagon until I say you can get up."

Reno lowered his daughter to the floor and she grabbed her bear, June, and went to her wagon in the corner of his office and lay down. She was quiet and motionless as she lay atop her pink and blue baby blanket. He'd debated many hours on how to break her off of the tattered blankie, and had come up with a solution. The blankie would disappear into the washer and never come out. But her mother had left the week of his plan, and the tattered material became Chloe's connection to the past along with June. Now, a year later, he'd gotten her to move the blankie from her bedroom to his office, and he hoped to drop it in the trash after Christina arrived.

With a last look at his too-quiet daughter, Reno sat down and folded the brochures of bedroom furniture he'd been researching for the girls. He liked the light mahogany. It was sturdy furniture they'd have all through middle school and then they'd probably want to redecorate.

Should they share a room or not? The house was a four bedroom, with the master suite on the main floor, a small nursery down the hall from the elegant bedroom. Chloe used to sleep upstairs, but she didn't want to be far from him since her mother had left, and he'd gotten tired of the awful fights they'd have when he tried to tuck her in each night.

She'd stopped talking, but had gotten him to listen. Each day she'd bring another bear down to the nursery and leave it there. When he or Mrs. Teralyn tried to put her down for a nap, she'd go to the nursery and lay on the floor.

One day he'd been flipping through the TV menu and stopped at the baby channel. The topic had been on understanding the needs of your newborn.

It had taken two weeks of awful crying fits, but Reno had finally gotten his daughter's message. Piece by piece, he'd taken apart the furniture from her upstairs bedroom, and Chloe, one bear at a time, helped him move her stuff down the hall from his room.

Rubbing his eyes, Reno pulled the folder of the potential wives in front of him. He read the demographic sheet of the first prospect. She was a one-hundred percent match. Thirty-five, never married, loved pets and children. Drug and background checks were clean.

She worked as a regional director for a

pharmaceutical company but wanted to leave the fast-paced career and settle down. An alarm bell rang in his head and Reno studied her photo. Why would an attractive, successful woman want to get involved with a man like him in his situation unless she was looking for more?

This was a temporary assignment. She either had a long list of demands, wanted more money like Isabelle, or wanted something permanent. He hadn't offered love, nor was he expecting it. All he wanted was marriage and a commitment to stay in the relationship a year until all the adoption paperwork was final. And for her trouble and confidence, the woman would be nicely compensated.

He carefully studied the other two demographic sheets and noted questions on a piece of paper when the doorbell rang.

Reno stood, suddenly nervous, although he'd just delved into the innermost part of these women's lives.

Straightening his clothes, he stopped when he heard a familiar voice.

Trina walked in with Mrs. Teralyn. "Hey." She gave him a quick hug. "Don't you look nice. I had to park in Spain and hike to your house."

"Why?" The atmosphere had changed with Trina's arrival. She was light to a dull day. Although the sun shined outside, it now brightened his office.

Trina got comfortable, setting her purse down in a chair. "I don't know. Surveyors are out there. Cable and somebody else."

"That's right. The house across the street has

been without utilities for a few days. They were struck by lightning during the last storm."

"Well, there are trucks blocking your driveway and the street alongside your house. I parked around the corner. You're walking me out, if you don't mind."

"I don't," he said.

She was a whirlwind and he loved her energy.

She regarded him. "You didn't have to get all dressed up for me."

"I didn't."

Behind Trina's back Mrs. Teralyn pointed at her and gave him the thumbs up.

"I'm offended." Trina roamed in an elegant black and white suit that gave away her womanly secrets. "Those new pants aren't for me and neither is the jacket."

"I always dress nice when I'm with you." Reno looked down at himself. "How did you know my slacks are new?"

She'd been looking at his books on the power of recycling rubber when she came around his desk and ripped the sticky tag off the side of his pant leg.

"This little indicator means they were ironed before you got them home, and you're lazy."

Reno laughed and peeled the size label off her finger, noting her red polish. Goodness, he loved red fingernails.

"Lazy. Hardly," he said, her perfume tickling his nose. "I've been busy."

Trina parked herself on the corner of his desk. "I hope you're working that brain on my behalf because I've been busy, too. I know you made your millions this morning between five and nine, so now that it's nine-fifty-ish, you can focus all your attention on me."

"I would love to." Reno sat in his brown high-boy leather chair and immediately realized his mistake. He was practically lick-level with Trina's legs. His manhood jumped.

He had a serious weakness for long, bronzed, pretty legs, and gorgeous feet.

Taking his eyes off them wasn't an option.

As her leg swung invitingly, his thoughts turned salacious.

She finally slid her hand down below her knee, her red painted nails luring his gaze up her leg and stomach, over the curve of her breast to her neck, and finally to her lips. "Are you enjoying the view?"

A growl started low in his gut and worked its way up his chest. "Best live wet dream I've ever almost had."

There was nothing on his desk except the folder of potential wives and the one woman he couldn't convince to be his wife. Reno had dreamed of her long beautiful legs last night. He'd gotten hard thinking about how it would feel to drag his hand over the mound of her bottom and down the back of her thigh. He'd take his time as he cupped her calf then caress her all the way to her ankle where he'd kiss her foot. He had a thing for pretty painted toes and well-maintained feet, and Trina's feet were as impeccable as her mind.

He couldn't resist, he had to touch her just once today. Yesterday's kiss prodding him to take more.

He didn't ask or wait for a reply, he put both hands on her legs and pulled her in front of him.

The folder fell to the floor and he heard the glossy photos scatter. They were crumbs compared with the delectable feast before him.

"Reno Merriwether, what are you doing?" Was that breathlessness he heard?

"If you don't know, then you shouldn't have wasted all the high school years on book learnin'"

She laughed at his 'Bama slang, her gaze searching, but not stopping him.

He tested the mettle of her temperament and ran his hands up the outside of her thighs.

"You're doing things to me I haven't thought about doing in a while." She sounded breathy and open to being seduced.

"I should stop then. I made you a promise last night. I wouldn't kiss you again."

Her perfectly arched brow curved up as if directed by a calligrapher. Everything in him said to make her his right now. But he'd promised not to kiss her.

Reno was a man of his word, but he knew he'd choose them more carefully next time. He let his hands do what his lips couldn't. As gentle as a butterfly, he stroked the inside of her left knee and it jerked. Reno caught her foot before it bruised his precious jewels.

Trina gasped, low and sexy. Her foot was perched between his thighs and he wondered if he could get her to grant him greater access.

Her foot wavered under the guidance of his gentle touch and he prayed like barren land for rain that she would open the portal that would give him the answers he sought.

"Kiss me there," she whispered.

Her words released the cylinder of his self-control and Reno bent, his lips barely making contact.

"Shoot!" Trina exclaimed, and kneed Reno in the mouth as she pushed off his desk.

His lip stung and his libido was confused. "What the hell just happened?"

Trina pointed.

Chloe was standing by the desk holding June in the air. She must have brushed Trina's hand with the bear.

His desire flat-lined. Trina had shot off the desk to a corner of his office where she discreetly fixed her skirt, although nothing was wrong with it.

"I'm sorry. She scared me. She's so quiet."

"That she is. That's—"

"I'm Trina." Taking tentative steps, Trina extended her hand to shake. She was treating his daughter as if she were a big girl.

Chloe looked at Trina's hand. Reno didn't believe anyone had ever tried to shake her hand before. He'd shown her how to high-five, but that was the extent of her social skills. Chloe didn't like strangers, either. She was known for walking off, getting her bear, and sitting down next to her parents. He and his ex had attributed it to her having been on lots of look-sees in the orphanage in Somalia, but they were never sure.

"Trina, Chloe doesn't know how to shake—"

Reno stopped talking as Chloe inched closer and shyly slid her chin into Trina's hand.

Trina knelt down and caressed Chloe's cheek with her thumb. "Well, aren't you a sweet girl?"

Chloe nodded.

Reno held his breath, watching his daughter

and the seductive woman he wanted as his own. Chloe never let anyone touch her. She just stood there for a minute and then slowly touched Trina's hair.

Trina looked at Reno and he shrugged. He couldn't believe what he was seeing.

A loud knock sounded and a woman walked into his office, her gaze openly inquisitive and suspicious as she took in the whole scene.

"Hi. I'm Felicity Davison, and you must be Reno Merriwether. Your housekeeper let me in. She said she's on her way to her doctor's appointment and she should be back in about two hours."

Reno stood and reached for Felicity's hand. He found her voice a bit loud and judgmental. "Thank you. I am Reno. Come on in." Felicity looked about five-five, with straight dark hair and wide-set eyes that revealed every thought. He didn't want to think of the dark-skinned woman as combative, but he got the impression she wouldn't back down when it came to stating her opinion. Unfortunately, right now he needed a wife, not a sparring partner.

Felicity eyed Trina and Chloe before confronting Reno. "Is there a reason why my picture's on the floor?"

Caught by surprise, Reno had forgotten about the photos and the folder. He quickly picked them up.

"They slipped off a few seconds ago. How are you?"

Felicity openly stared at Trina, seeming to take inventory of her clothes and jewelry, and then of her as a woman. She seemed curious about them and he wondered if she'd ask or just assume.

She didn't acknowledge Chloe who stood between Reno and Trina looking like she would spring at him at any second.

Reno saw June the bear in Chloe's hands and wished he hadn't let her nap so early. Now she wouldn't go to sleep for hours. And having Chloe in his lap might not go over well with the potential wives, especially on the first visit.

"Is she in the running?" Felicity asked, jutting her chin in Trina's direction.

"No." Trina looked at Reno, then away. She rose and the woman followed every inch of Trina's figure as she stood to her full height in heels. She admired her beauty, he could tell, but she was also intimidated, and if she were in Reno's life, she'd try to make him choose, even in a false marriage of convenience.

Trina was silent as she let the woman stare at her. She didn't care what Felicity thought, he realized. She wasn't bothered by jealousy or the fact that she'd inadvertently turned him down again. Trina just was. She'd always been honest with him about everything.

Alluring, intelligent, and fearless. He hadn't found more appealing qualities in any woman. Thinking of her while she endured Felicity's scrutiny reminded him of his earlier attempt at seduction. Just the thought of her letting him have his way with her increased his libido. Mentally he doused the flame. Now wasn't the time to be thinking about how he'd take her.

Felicity dropped her hands to her hips, showing off a well-toned body and nice hair. Yet her pouty mouth was pointed at him.

"I'm applying for the temporary position as your wife. Is this for some kind of play or something? Because I don't really understand why you need a wife with *her* around."

"Trina's a friend of the family. My situation is delicate. Please, sit down."

Reno had initially planned to have the meeting at the coffee table and chairs across the room, but with Trina and Chloe standing in the office and not leaving, he wasn't sure what to do. "Would you like something to drink?" Reno offered.

"I could take some black tea, hot. *Hot,*" Felicity emphasized to Trina, over her shoulder. She then turned around. "Cream, one sugar."

Trina gave Reno an indignant glare over Felicity's head and started from the office.

He pushed his chair back, waiting for Chloe who was still rooted in the same place since before Felicity walked in.

Trina got to the door and turned around. "Chloe?"

His daughter's head snapped around.

"Want to help me?"

Chloe shook her head no. She walked in a wide path around the desk, stuck her foot in the handle of the desk, then the arm of the chair, climbed up and finally sat into her father's lap.

"Reno, anything for you?" Trina asked.

Her voice did things to him and to be safe he didn't look at her.

"No, thanks. I appreciate this—" he began to say, but she waved him off.

When he couldn't hear her heels anymore he turned back to Felicity.

"Your resume is impressive. How long have you been in pharmaceuticals?"

"Nine years. Listen, they've already done a background check on both of us, so we can rehash the details of our resumes or I can find out what it is you really want."

Her candor wasn't expected, but Felicity had a point. "I need a wife to adopt my d-a-u-g-h-t-e-r's s-i-s-t-e-r."

Chloe turned around, stuck her finger in his mouth and tried to pry it open.

"Ms. Little lady? Please stop or you're going to go lie down in the wagon."

Chloe got a sad face and sat down.

"Why is she so quiet?" Felicity sounded accusing.

Trina walked in unobtrusively and served them tea. She'd put two small cookies on a napkin for Chloe and made sure everyone had everything before going to the back of the room and sitting down on the couch.

"I mean," Felicity said, in a less aggressive tone, "Can she speak at all?"

"Yes, and one day she will again," Reno said, not liking Felicity much.

"What does that mean? Can she talk or not?"

"She can talk. However, she's been through a lot and she's not talking right now."

Chloe wiped the top of the cookie with her little thumb, over and over again. Crumbs landed on her dress, and had she been a normal healthy child, he'd have scooped her up and taken her to the table to eat.

But he'd seen this before. This was Chloe's expression of being nervous. She didn't like Felicity either.

"I'm pretty good with kids," Felicity said, her brows furrowed. "I'll make her talk."

The cookie broke.

"Thank you, Felicity. I'm sorry to cut our time short, but I have two additional interviews and the next one will be here in five minutes."

She sat forward and looped her arm in her purse straps. She hadn't even sipped the tea she'd just scooped four sugars into. "Okay then." She reached for Reno's hand. "Thank you. I look forward to hearing from you soon."

Trina was at the door by the time Felicity got up. "I'll show you out," she said and gave Reno a professional smile.

Reno looked down at his daughter whose eyes were filled with tears. "Hey, it's just a cookie. Do you want another one?"

She shook her head no.

"Well then, let's get rid of the crumbs from this one. I think you need a swing." He cupped her in his arms and pretended to swing her all the way to the kitchen sink. He stood her on the edge, careful she wasn't unsteady and slowly poofed out her dress so the crumbs fell into the sink.

"Brush off your hands, Chloe."

She looked at them and the tears that had threatened to fall did. "It's okay, baby. It's just a cookie."

She shook her head no, and Reno felt the guessing game begin. It often took an hour for him to figure out what was wrong with her and he just didn't have time today. If Mrs. Teralyn had been there, she'd have kept up a running monologue to which Chloe wouldn't have had to respond. Somehow the grandmother of ten knew what Chloe needed right away.

Reno pulled down a paper towel and sat Chloe on the counter. "Do you want another cookie?"

She shook her head no.

"Juice?"

Again, another shake.

"Pizza with cheese for lunch?"

She shook her head slowly, looking up at him, a question in her eyes.

"Come on, Chloe," he said, wiping her baby finger. "Tell Daddy what you want."

She opened her mouth and his heart thundered.

"She's gone," Trina said, walking into the kitchen.

Chloe's lips closed and she peeked around his shoulder at Trina.

The anticipation sank to the bottom of his stomach like a ton of rocks.

He hugged Chloe and she automatically put her arms around his neck for him to carry her. Reno thought of putting her down, but knew if her feet touched the floor in front of Trina, she'd have a tantrum, and after this morning, he wasn't up for another so soon.

"Ready, little miss?"

Chloe nodded.

"Trina," he said finally, looking at her. "Do you want to go over your plan?"

She folded her hands. "Sure. I didn't like her

either. I put everything on a flash drive and I printed it for us to review together. But you don't need me here to review. You can read it and get back to me at your convenience."

"You in a rush," he asked, walking back to his office.

"No. I assumed you blocked out some time for me. I brought some bagels so you wouldn't be hungry while you pored over my stuff."

Flattered, he lowered Chloe to the rug, and immediately moved to pick her up, she was so close to Trina, but Chloe walked to the patio door and stared out.

For a while they watched the little girl, who didn't move or make a sound.

"It has to break your heart." Trina stroked his back.

He wanted to share his hopes and dreams, his desires for his daughters and his plans for the future. He always imagined a wife to talk to about these things, but with no one to talk to, he felt strangely incomplete.

Early this morning he'd found himself looking at colleges for the girls. Reno kept silent. He hadn't been silent with Trina last night. She'd prodded his thoughts from his soul and now that the well was open, he felt like overflowing.

Besides his unplanned kiss last night, they officially were just friends, and although he wanted things to be different, they weren't.

"Let's take a look at the plans," Reno offered. "What's up for this week?"

"A cook-off at a cooking school."

His eyebrows shot up. "For ladies and men?"

"Of course, silly," Trina said. "Doesn't that sound like fun?"

He didn't want to burst her bubble. "Uh," he chuckled while putting Felicity's photo in the shred folder in his desk. "Yeah, for a group of lesbians. Or gay men."

Trina looked surprised and he couldn't help wanting to kiss her mouth. She walked over to his bookshelf and flipped through a fifty-page article on the advantages of recycling plastic bottles into medical equipment. She picked up the bound pages and walked around with them.

"Cooking isn't just for gays and lesbians. It's for everybody," Trina explained. "The clients can have fun, making a dish, talking. Getting to know one another."

"Okay. I'll play devil's advocate here. What if nobody shows up?"

"They'll show up, Reno. This will be fun."

"So your electronic sign-up sheet is full? Let me access it. Where's your flash pin?"

"I don't have an electronic sign up sheet."

"You have to have that in case they send out an auditor."

"I know, but something ate it up and my cousins are working on it."

"That sounds a little odd, don't you think?"

"Reno, computers break all the time."

"Yeah, but do they gobble up one thing or everything?"

Trina's hand slapped her mouth.

"Tell me you changed your passwords after Drake and Nona left."

"I did for Nona, but not Drake. Sh—" she

began, and he silenced her with a finger to his lips. "You'll have to pay up."

Trina sat on the side of his desk and mouthed the curse words.

Reno laughed. Her hands were balled up, her nose was turning red and the vein at the top of her head popped out.

"Do you think he's still backstabbing me? I let it go concerning the interview and giving up my confidential schedule. But this? He'll wish he never met me." She pulled her cell phone from her Prada purse and stabbed the keypad.

Reno covered her hands and shook them until she looked at him.

"I know you Crawfords get away with a lot of stuff here in Georgia, but I don't think calling the family hit man is the answer."

"I was calling Jade, my aunt who's a bounty hunter. She knows people."

"Okay, Trina *Soprano*. It's not that serious. You told me before that your system backs everything up every night."

"It does."

Her eyes turned to the color of the distant sea.

"Your eyes are blue."

"Not really. My top's blue. Makes my eyes blue if I'm angry."

"So many secrets for one long lady."

She tilted her head. "I thought you were going to say little, and then I'd know you were bullshitting me."

"Pay up. A dollar."

She reached inside her purse and laid a gold

coin in his hand. He opened the bottom desk drawer and dropped it in the jug.

Her mouth pitched up in a half smile and he felt guilty. "Who's all that?"

"I'm sure you can guess. Call Tracey and tell her to change the password."

Trina did as instructed and closed her phone.

"Okay, let's get back to the schedule. I was thinking happy hours, building houses." He looked at a list he'd scribbled last night when he couldn't sleep. "That was good. I'm thinking picnic."

"In March? The weather is too unpredictable."

"Concert at Lakewood." Reno snapped his fingers and Chloe stepped sideways so she could see him.

"Nothing, baby. You can look out the window."

She stared at him for a while, picked up June, and got in her wagon. Flipping over she faced the wall.

Trina watched the chain of events with a mixture of sympathy and shock.

"I have no idea what to do with a depressed child."

Startled by what he just said, Reno looked for something with which to busy his hands. He'd never thought of Chloe as being depressed. He wasn't even aware that little children could be depressed. Why had he said that?

"Where's the flash drive?" he asked.

Trina watched him for a moment, then retrieved it from her briefcase.

"I shouldn't have said that. I'm not a doctor."

"Reno, we as a society need not shove depression under the rug. My cousin is going through a depression."

"How old is he or she?"

"She's thirty-one."

"That's hardly the same."

"I'm sorry. I shouldn't have drawn a comparison. I'm no expert either," Trina said.

"Okay," he replied sharper than he intended. He took a second and found his voice. "I'm doing the best that I can. I don't know what to do with her. I love her, feed and clothe her. I can't believe Dana left her daughter. What kind of mother does that?" He whispered so Chloe couldn't hear and searched for answers in Trina's eyes. All he saw was the sea.

"Dana trusts you, Reno." She let her words sink in, her gaze convincing him to believe her. "She knew you were the better parent, so she wasn't selfish. She left her in good hands. Your hands."

Her words healed sores he didn't know he still had. He'd never considered that Dana had given him this much credit. He thought she'd been selfish for leaving them and pursuing a life of her own. What she'd been was generous.

The cancerous anger that had kept him from forgiving Dana slipped away on an empty breath. He'd been so hurt that she'd left him, he hadn't examined the reasons why she'd left Chloe with him.

Hundreds of days had passed, had he taken himself out of the equation, and then he may have been able to find a way to help his daughter.

Trina was still looking at him, confusion in her

eyes right before her face became a mask. He couldn't allow her to retreat.

"Reno, I shouldn't have—"

He stroked the back of her hand, then kissed it. Her skin was softer than the velvet cape she'd worn. He'd made a promise to not kiss her again, but he found himself breaking his own rule again.

"You're right. I'd never thought of it that way and I wished I hadn't wasted so much time. Okay?"

She seemed to be trying to gauge him. "Okay," she finally said.

Let's see if we can retrieve this list." His cell phone rang and he hesitated, then picked it up. "Reno Merriwether."

"Mr. Merriwether, this is Mrs. Elmi from the Mandela Agency regarding the impending adoption. We wanted to know if we could tell the court that you will definitely be coming in four weeks."

"Four? I thought I had six?" Holding the phone to his ear, he opened the drawer and pulled out his electronic organizer. Manipulating the wand, he reviewed his calendar. "I do have six weeks. What's going on?"

"Well things have been pushed up because new laws will soon take effect that will make it harder for Americans to adopt African children. Please, Sir. Can you give me an answer today?"

Reno paced. He didn't have a wife. He'd be wasting his time, but he couldn't leave his daughter's sister in an orphanage. Without knowing her he already loved her.

"Yes, Mrs. Elmi. We'll be there."

"Will there be three or four traveling with you?"

This was the tricky part. He didn't know. "Four."

"Sir, I need the names. I have to submit them on a document to the court."

"The first name is Reno Merriwether. Chloe Merriwether."

The doorbell rang and Trina got up, her expression serious. Across the room their eyes met and then he looked at his sleeping daughter.

"Gwendolyn Teralyn. I'll have the other name this evening. Good-bye," he said, and hung up. "Trina, I need your help. Can you help me?"

Chapter 9

Trina's tongue stuck to the roof of her mouth. She wanted to run for the door, but Reno's gaze kept her rooted to her seat. "Sure. I'll help you."

Please don't propose. Please don't propose. She didn't want to break his heart or hers. She'd been feeling emotional every time she'd been around him. He'd been her rock and sounding board, and during the wee hours when she'd been updating the website, she'd mulled every piece of advice he'd given her, and had to admit her company was better for his foresight.

But were the feelings that left her thinking of him love?

Back in college she'd had to work for his attention, and no matter how much she'd wanted to get past his personal barricade, his denial was as strong as the picks he set in basketball games.

She'd been young, and her life as a Crawford had always softened rejection, but when she'd gone to college and met Reno, she'd known instantly he had the ability to hurt her deeply by not giving her the one thing she'd wanted, and that was him.

For the first time in her life the fear of rejection kept her from laying her heart on the line.

So she'd taken what he'd given, his attention at helping her meet her goal in basketball, and she'd learned the benefit of hard work.

So what if Reno wanted a marriage in name only? She could do that for a couple months after all he'd done for her. Nothing would be expected of her emotionally. But that was the problem. Now that they'd reconnected, her feelings for him had grown to more than just acquaintances from the past.

She'd want to help him with the girls, and she didn't understand children at all. They'd be on Dr. Phil in four months.

The image of Chloe standing between them as she probably had with her parents filled her with sadness. No child should have to choose.

Trina's heart went out to the little girl as she rubbed her tingling palm. She still couldn't believe that after all she knew about Chloe, she'd allowed Trina to touch her.

Despite having been adopted, Chloe and her father resembled each other in coloring and their eyes were the same. At the moment, her expression was stressed, just like her dad's.

The question stuck to Trina's lips and she knew she'd give the answer he wanted if he asked her again. Reno had done too much for her to say no, but he had to ask. She'd already gone beyond her limits by sitting on his desk and encouraging him to kiss her knees. That was only one of her erogenous zones.

He made her feel safe and vulnerable and ready to explore the next natural step.

He was changing her. Turning her into a seductress, a woman who had carnal needs that were surfacing, like lava to the earth's surface.

She kept reminding herself that he needed someone who would make his family whole again.

Toying with him was inexcusable.

Reno hadn't changed what he wanted, but she was changing, and that wasn't fair to him. He deserved to find someone who would complete his family and make them whole again. If she had to be that for the short term, then she would.

Taking a deep breath, her shoulders dropped. "What do you need?"

"Will you get the door?"

She felt as if her heart had been trampled by a dozen hooves. "Yes, of course."

She grabbed her purse and started up the hallway, trying to catch her breath.

"Trina?"

Reno was behind her and if he reached out she'd melt into his arms. "Yes?"

"Were you saying yes to something else?"

"Excuse me?" She knew exactly what he was talking about, but if he didn't ask . . .

"Were you saying yes—"

The doorbell rang.

"I'd better get that and be on my way."

"I need you," he said.

She heard fast, heavy breathing, and she realized Chloe was crying without making a sound.

Trina stepped toward her, but Reno picked her up and Trina hurried to get the door.

"Trina, please stay. Mrs. Teralyn will be back soon, and then we can talk. Please," Reno said. "I can't do this by myself."

"I can't." She'd almost scooped up the child to comfort her.

Trina pulled open the front door and a stylish dark-skinned black woman walked in. She offered her hand. "I'm Heidi Webb to see Reno Merriwether."

"Pleased to meet you. Trina Crawford. Please come in. This is Reno Merriwether and his daughter, Chloe. I was just leaving."

Chloe bucked and flailed against her father, the silent tantrum bizarre.

"Didn't we talk about this, Chloe?" Reno said with more calm than Trina thought any man other than her father capable of. "You're going to go to your room."

Chloe acted like she didn't hear him. She continued to flail.

Heidi looked horrified. "Is she special needs? Because nobody ever said anything about that."

"And if she is?" Reno asked.

"Then I'd thank you for your time. I'm not the woman for you."

"Chloe," Trina jumped in, not understanding why she hadn't run out the open door minutes ago. She put down her purse. "I think there are some ducks outside. Let's go take a look."

Chloe was arched backwards, and Reno gave Trina the wiggling heap of child. "You can take her over to the pond. She likes it there, but we haven't gone in a while. It's across the street behind those homes. Just follow the path," he told her, sounding as somber as he looked.

He kissed his daughter's forehead, draped Trina's purse strap on her shoulder and escorted the potential Mrs. Merriwether to his office.

Trina walked out the front door and carried the sprawled child outside, not knowing what to do with her.

As soon as the front door closed, Chloe stopped fighting. She just lay limp in Trina's arms.

Trina soothed Chloe as she walked down the winding flat stairs to the sidewalk where she readjusted her to fit snugly against her body as she'd done with younger cousins a thousand times.

Looking at Chloe's precious face, Trina was awed by her loveliness, but she was still shocked that Chloe didn't make a sound.

Sorrow wound its way through Trina's chest as Chloe sucked up unspent tears.

"You know, my mom made up a song for me because I cried so much."

Trina waited for the little girl to look at her and she did, her brown eyes fatigued.

"When the song didn't work, Mama would pretend like she was crying and I would stop because I didn't want Mama to cry."

Chloe wiped her face and looked at her hand. She shook it to get the tears off. When her hand didn't dry she held it out to Trina.

"They're tears, sweet girl." She kissed Chloe's hand and looked both ways before crossing the street.

A short path led them to the pond where

spring had blossomed. Bright and colorful petunias, begonias and daisies had been planted in a lovely floral paradise.

The mild day had brought lots of mothers to the pond where they pushed their children in strollers, and gave kids bread to feed the ducks.

Hearing a puppy, Chloe scrambled up from her protected position in Trina's arms. She stared at it and pointed.

"Pup-py. Can you say puppy?"

Chloe shook her head no. She watched from high up as the happy animal loped through a little boy's legs, playing. He giggled, chasing the dog.

Trina strolled in the direction of a large group of ducks.

"Can you say my name? It's Trina."

Chloe's lips didn't move, but her eyes missed nothing. Trina knew she was taking everything in, but for some reason had decided she wasn't being heard, so she'd shut down.

She felt protective of the child and wanted to cuddle her closely, but Chloe moved anxiously, her heartbeat thumping.

They settled on a bench and Trina took off her jacket. "It's going to be a pretty summer. Do you have a swimming suit?"

Chloe sat next to her in her pretty pink and white dress, her hair braided in two ponytails. "I have ten swimming suits," she told Chloe.

The little girl shrugged again and Trina laughed. "You're right. Who cares?" She crossed her legs and Chloe scrambled up to see what she was doing. "I need to clean out my closet," she told Chloe, "Maybe Suddenlysingleatl.com can do a clothing drive."

Trina pulled a single roll of M&Ms from her purse. Her one tiny indulgence.

"Can you have candy?"

Chloe shrugged.

"You have to know something." Trina broke one of the candies in half and put it in Chloe's hand. She didn't want to upset her by trying to feed it to her. Trina ate the other half and was glad when Chloe did the same.

"You like it?"

Chloe shrugged, her face twisting into a frown as she chewed.

"Who doesn't like candy?" Trina asked her. "You're going to have to get out more. They've kept you bottled up too long if you don't know about candy. Uh oh, here come the ducks. They must have heard the paper rattling."

As the sea of white squawking ducks approached, Chloe kneeled next to Trina, then climbed over her hip, clutching Trina's head. Trina tried to peel Chloe off, but she held on until she landed in Trina's lap.

Trina covered Chloe with her jacket. "Honey, they aren't going to bother you. They're just hungry. Shoo ducks!" she said, stamping her foot. "Go away. Ya! Ya!"

The ducks scampered toward a woman with a bag of bread.

Trina looked under her jacket at the scared little girl. "You're safe. They're gone." Chloe just looked at Trina.

How could Reno stand it? Chloe had retreated

from the world. She didn't laugh or talk or respond beyond a shrug. How could anyone know
how she felt? What if Chloe needed something?
Reno had to be stressed out from having to guess
at everything.

Her heart broke for the little girl with expressive
dark eyes and a beautiful heart-shaped face.

Trina closed her jacket a tiny bit, but Chloe
could still see her. "Where's Chloe?" Trina asked,
pretending to look around. "Chloe, girl? Where
are you?"

Chloe's braid came undone and she wiped her
hair from her eyes and peeked out. She blinked
rapidly at Trina, though Trina pretended not to
see her.

"I don't see Chloe," she said, looking all
around. "Where is she? Oh, boo-hoo."

Chloe's forehead and nose popped out of the
jacket, and Trina pretended not to see her. "I
miss Chloe. Will she come out and play with
me?"

Chloe's whole face came out of the jacket and
she cupped Trina's face so they were looking at
each other. "Here you are!" she said excited. "I'm
so happy to see you. Oh, Chloe. Can I have a hug?"

Trina held out her arms and waited. Chloe hesitated and then wrapped her arms around Trina's
neck and squeezed as tight as her little arms
could. Then she patted Trina on the back, com-
forting her.

Tears rushed to Trina's eyes as she waited for
Chloe to let her go first. She was indeed the
sweetest little girl ever.

When she didn't let go, Trina held on for as

long as it took a cloud to free the sun, the ducks to come and go again, and the little girl to gently pat love into Trina's back with her tiny little hand.

Finally, Chloe let her go and played with Trina's hair. Trina fished in her purse for a tissue and dabbed her tears as Chloe stood on the bench, the ducks forgotten. She pointed to her hiding place.

"You were right here," Trina said, as she pocketed her damp tissue. "You're the best surprise ever. Come on. Let's look at those flowers."

Trina eyed her watch. The work on her desk wasn't going to do itself. She'd already been here longer than she'd anticipated, but how could she tell Reno that paperwork was more important than finding a mother for his daughter? She and Chloe walked the pond twice before Trina, in her high heels, gave up. She sat down and crossed her legs.

Chloe did the same, even mimicking Trina's folded fingers.

Trina looked at Chloe's shoes. Black patent leather with silver buckles. They were cute and flat.

"I like your shoes," Trina told her.

Chloe shrugged and nodded her head.

"Chloe?"

She looked up at Trina.

"Can you say my name?"

Chloe shook her head no.

"It's not hard. I'm Trina and you're Chloe," she said pointing. "Trina. Chloe. Trina. Chloe. Now you try."

"Trina," Trina said slowly to help Chloe, who watched her mouth.

When it was evident Chloe wasn't going to respond, they walked again with Chloe picking up damaged flowers until they had a bouquet.

A couple of flowers were broken too close to the bud, so Trina made shoe decorations and pushed one into the top of Chloe's shoe and one into hers. "I wish I had a pair of shoes like yours. Don't wear heels when you're grown," Trina advised. "If you start wearing them, you'll become dependent." Trina covered her mouth. "Are you going to tell on me?"

Chloe shrugged, then shook her head no.

"Good, because I'm in the market for a new best friend. Would you like to apply?"

Trina anticipated her shrug and nudged Chloe who smiled and moved right back next to Trina. "I know, you don't care. You're a great candidate because you don't talk. Actually, you're the best kind of friend to have."

Chloe shrugged and Trina rubbed her back. "It's getting late. If you know the way home, I'll follow you."

Chloe took Trina's hand and they retraced their steps all the way back to the street across from the house and Chloe pointed. "Home."

Trina's mouth fell open. She grabbed Chloe into her arms and spun her around.

"You talked! Say it again."

Chloe didn't and pointed to the house.

Her glee slipped away, replaced by anger.

What in the hell was Nona's car doing in Reno's driveway?

Chapter 10

What was that backstabbing weasel doing here? She couldn't have been one of Reno's potential wives.

Which meant she was up to no good.

Lifting Chloe into her arms, Trina strode across the street and through the unlocked front door.

"I'm not interested in working for you." Trina slowed when she heard Reno say this. "My loyalties are to Trina. I'm sorry you don't get that."

Trina paused and put her finger to her lips telling Chloe to stay quiet. The girl didn't move.

"We could be partners," Nona said, sounding flirty. "Whatever she's giving you, I can beat."

"I thought you were partners with Drake?" Reno sounded bored.

"We satisfy each other's more carnal needs." Nona was playing her hand. But why? According to her, Trina had stolen everything from her. And if there was any truth to Nona's media mouthpiece Leeza, and their website, she was beating the crap out of Trina in the competition. So why was she here trying to take something else that wasn't hers?

"Drake can't keep my juices flowing, personally or professionally. We're professional acquaintances," she clarified for Reno. "To be honest, I understand why Trina dumped him. He's a little too effeminate for my taste."

Nona made a shuddering noise.

"Does Drake know you're here?" Reno asked.

"Reno, I need a man on my team that's savvy, intelligent, and successful. I can give you exactly what you want."

Reno's chair rolled backwards. "This meeting is over."

"A mother so you can get your daughter's sister?"

"How do you know my business?"

"Felicity Davison is a client I recommended to the Hartford Agency."

"I met her. How did you know to send her here?"

Nona chuckled. "I had background checks performed on everyone in Trina's camp. I was gathering information and this nugget popped out about you."

A vertical shadow of Reno's body crept up the wall. "That's over the line." His voice was tight.

"But not illegal." Overconfidence made Nona sound nasal. "I'm glad I did it. You and I can meet each other's needs."

"While the SBO might not think it's illegal, it's nasty. Goodbye, Nona."

"Okay, I apologize. But you deserve to get what you want out of life too, Reno. Imagine how it will feel to have your girls together. When was the last time someone put you first?"

For a minute there was silence. "I don't know."

Trina's heart sank. She'd promised to help him, knowing he wanted the one thing she couldn't give. He'd known he was asking the impossible, but he was right. No one had put him first.

"You asked Trina, and she said no."

Reno didn't respond and Trina wanted to run in the room and tell him she'd do it, but she couldn't motivate herself.

"She's selfish." Nona's matter-of-fact tone beat on Trina's guilty conscience. "Nothing was ever more important than what she wanted. Last year I had to have my gall bladder removed. To this day she doesn't know because she never called me. I was always calling her. My mother's been sick for six months, and has Trina ever once asked me how she is? Not once. She's in a hospice, Reno. But Trina doesn't know that because I stopped talking about my mother and she never noticed."

"I'm sorry, Nona, but that doesn't make what you're doing with Drake right."

"Reno, I know everything about her family to the most ridiculous detail because they're all she talks about. She and Drake weren't the perfect couple. They were two narcissistic people in a superficial relationship. I didn't have to do more than be there to get him when it was over."

"People end friendships every day. You didn't have to handle your breakup with Trina this way."

"What way? Having my way, *finally*? I deserve success. Reno, you want something and I'm willing to give it to you. I would be there for you. Who knows, we might even decide to stay together afterwards."

Guilt at every truth Nona had hurled against Trina stung. Shame wasn't an emotion Trina was used to and all she wanted to do was run out the door and back to her old life—the life where she didn't think she had so many faults.

Chloe looked at her with innocent eyes, patted Trina on the back, and pointed to her dad's office. But Trina shook her head. She had to leave Reno alone for good.

"What are you offering?" Reno asked. The tears that sprang to Trina's eyes were hot and heavy. They slipped down her cheeks and Chloe wiped them.

Sadness had invaded Chloe and she looked like she was on the brink of tears, too.

Trina tried to pull herself together so that they both weren't blubbering messes when Chloe put her hand on Trina's chin and nudged her face up.

How had this baby endured so much? How much pain was she in to make her stop talking?

Trina couldn't help hugging her, and when Chloe's little arms gripped her neck, it took all of Trina's strength not to run into Reno's office and promise to be his wife.

But how could they both get what they wanted?

More to the point, when it was time, could she leave without damaging this child who was giving her something so unconditional that Trina had never consciously known existed?

"My daughter and housekeeper will be home soon. What are your terms?"

"I'll expect you to help me win this contest," Nona said, her excitement barely controlled. "We can get married right away and get to know one another so that we're authentic to the people you have to report to. Doesn't that sound good?"

"Yes, it does." Reno's words echoed in Trina's chest. Chloe's racing heartbeat matched Trina's.

Trina put Chloe on the floor and nudged her so she'd go to her father. She walked away slowly, then came back. Taking Trina's hand, she tried to pull her toward the office.

"No, sweetie. I have to go," Trina whispered. "Go to daddy, please."

Chloe stopped pulling her towards the office and looked out the window. At a loss for what to do, Trina bent down. "I'll be back, I promise." She didn't know how Dana had left this beautiful little girl behind.

Had she made promises and not kept them? Had she lied, or had she cared at all? Trina knew one thing. Her heart was breaking, and if this was love, it hurt like hell.

Opening her purse, she found a nearly empty tube of MAC lip gloss. She tightened the cap and gave it to Chloe. "Will you keep this for me until I come back?"

Chloe shrugged and accepted it.

"You make me work so hard, you little angel. Okay, put this in your wagon and lie down so daddy can finish talking, okay?"

Chloe shook her head no.

"Chloe, please talk for daddy like you did for me, remember? You said home. You knew exactly where your house was and you said home. Daddy will be so happy to hear your voice."

Chloe shrugged.

Trina kissed the back of Chloe's hand. "You're a sweet girl and I promise I'll come back to see you," she whispered, kissing Chloe's cheek, until she smiled. "Now go inside with Daddy."

She walked off with the tube of lip gloss, taking slow steps. When she was at the door, she looked back at Trina.

Trina urged her in, while backing up.

"Reno, I'll triple whatever Trina's paying you. The fringe benefits are worth it."

"Trina isn't paying me."

"Then she's taking advantage of you, knowing you're about to become a father again."

Trina couldn't hear any more. Chloe made it into her father's office.

"Hey, little girl," her dad said. "Where's—"

Trina saw him once he came into the doorway. She'd reached the front door. "I thought we were going to talk."

She couldn't see him through her tears, but she shook her head and turned the knob, opening the door.

"This isn't what you think," he said.

"Chloe said 'home'," Trina said softly.

"What?" Reno's gaze switched from Trina to Chloe. "Did you talk?"

Chloe shrugged and showed him the lipstick. Reno smiled, picking her up. "Did you talk today? Can you say something for Daddy?" He looked at her hand. "Where'd you get this?"

The tube slipped from Chloe's hand and rolled across the wood floor into the office.

"Why hello," Nona said, syrupy sweet. "Love Nectar. That's Trina's color. She's here? I didn't know it was like that between you two, Reno. That doesn't change my offer. In fact, why don't you interview us together for the position of Mrs. Merriwether? Could prove interesting."

"That won't be necessary."

Trina hurried around the corner and got into her car.

She started the BMW and drove away quickly, hating that she glanced in the rearview mirror, to see if he'd come after her. He had. With Chloe.

She *was* selfish. *Cruel.* And she was wrong.

She'd allowed Reno and Chloe to get to know her and now she was walking away when she'd known all along she couldn't give him what he wanted and what Chloe needed.

A memory of how it felt to hold Chloe close rushed into her, making her body ache. Trina knew she'd absolutely fallen in love with the little girl.

Nona had been right. Her relationship with Drake had been lifeless and fake, but that was only because she hadn't wanted to get close. She'd been so hell-bent on her career, that was the only type of relationship she'd wanted.

Now she'd gone and fallen in love with Chloe and her father, knowing she wouldn't do a damn thing about it.

Trina would swallow her tongue before admitting aloud that there was an ounce of truth to anything Nona had said, but she'd been right.

Stopping at a red light, Trina's tears fell into her lap and she pressed her palm to her jaw to stem the flow, but each time her hand remained wet, like Chloe's had been.

She took a watery breath and jumped when a car horn blasted behind her.

Trina pointed her car towards I-75 and headed to her office. She had a house to build and she and the rest of the Suddenlysingle staff had to be ready. Her tears stopped by the time she walked into her office and dropped her purse into her desk drawer. She would no longer play the modern day Florence Nightingale by trying to save everybody. No, she'd focus on what she really was. Selfish.

Chapter 11

Walking toward the Next Step construction houses that were under construction, Reno was glad that he had dressed for the warm weather in a short-sleeved blue T-shirt, jeans, and work boots.

Reno was proud of the number of volunteers demonstrated by the number of cars in the two full lots across the street from the homes.

But he questioned why he'd bothered to come. He hadn't talked to Trina in a week.

His tool belt felt odd in his hand, he hadn't carried it in so long, but it was a welcome difference to the keyboard he'd been typing on since he'd started his own business seven years ago. Today he was volunteering his services and he was glad to think of someone besides himself.

People were working hard on the houses and there were couples everywhere. This event was a hit for Trina.

He didn't see her, but there were Crawfords everywhere, making him wish he had a clan.

Tracey, Trina's cousin, sat at the command

post tent, two large fans blowing on her, and large sunglasses covering her face. She gave concise instructions, but didn't seem too enthused with anyone or anything.

Although they'd never exchanged more than a few words, he approached, determined to make her smile.

Standing in line, he waited his turn, his ID in his hand.

"Name?" she asked, looking at her sheet.

"Reno Merriwether."

She looked up and her mouth wavered. "Oh." Tracey blinked several times through the tan lenses and she didn't say anything for a few seconds. "You're not on the list. I compiled it myself, and I know without looking at it that you're not on it."

"Does that mean I can't get on it?" he asked with a smile.

"No," she said quietly.

"I'd like to be your friend, Tracey. Trina talks about you all the time."

"She doesn't have a choice. We share the same blood type."

Reno pointed at her. "You're funny. May I have a badge?"

She slapped the list closed and grabbed a permanent marker and sticky badge. "Sure. R-e-n-o. Right?"

"Yep. Cause R-i-n-o would be a whole different species."

She stopped writing. "Sorry," he said. Taking a different approach, he walked around the table and sat down next to her, laying his tool belt by his feet.

"You aren't supposed to be back here. I don't know the status of your relationship with my cousin, so I don't know how to treat you."

"Why not judge for yourself and just be my friend? Hi, I'm Reno Merriwether. And you are?"

"Tracey Crawford. We can't be friends. You mean something to my cousin and my allegiance belongs to her."

Despite his best effort to be unaffected, he couldn't stop that dart from hurting. "Okay. It's a nice day and I thought I'd try to make a friend. It's been nice talking to you, Tracey."

"Wait. That wasn't right at all. I'm sorry. I don't have a lot of friends so I can use one or two. I'm Tracey Anne Crawford. Thirty-one."

Reno sat back down. "What's your story, Tracey? You're the saddest girl here. And, I want to add that you're one of the prettiest. I'm totally into your cousin," he said, "So don't take what I said the wrong way. I'm just wondering why you don't ever smile."

She did smile, but it ended in a watery grave of tears. "I met someone a few months ago and we were doing very well, and then he changed. Now he can't see me. He can't come by because I live too far. He's tense, stressed, argumentative, and unavailable. He needed money to help him out of a jam and I loaned it to him."

Reno tried to hide his cringe, but she saw it. Tracey played with her fingers just like Trina. He took her hand. "How much?" he asked.

"Three—"

"Please don't say thousand."

"I'm not totally stupid. Three hundred dollars."

"Is that it?" Reno asked.

"I think he might be seeing someone else," Tracey said softly. "A man."

Reno nodded. "Okay. First things first. If you only lost three hundred dollars, that's not your life savings, so you're good there. Second, and don't take this the wrong way, but have you had an HIV/AIDS test?"

"No. That's what's got my head so messed up. I have to get one for my own peace of mind." She sat forward and pressed the heel of her hand into her forehead. "We were talking about getting married. I thought I'd hit the relationship lottery. I naturally assumed that it was okay to go without protection."

Reno pulled a small piece of paper and his carpenter's pencil from his tool belt and wrote down a number.

"I travel a lot, and this doctor's office is always accommodating when it comes to getting immunizations I need. I'm sure they can handle any test that needs to be done. They're fast and discreet."

Trina rounded the corner and Reno saw her. He rose, refraining from going to her.

"Doctor Oglethorpe does great work on bunions. You shouldn't have any problem getting an appointment. Just tell him I referred you."

Tracey looked left, saw Trina, and then back at Reno. "Thanks. Trina, we have two hundred sixteen volunteers. They've been split equally between both houses."

"Why? We decided on one house last week."

"Yes, but with all the volunteers coming today we decided to get started on both today."

Trina wouldn't look at Reno. "Nobody consulted me."

"You're right Trina, we didn't. You were gone all day yesterday and when I called this morning, you didn't answer. Today, you were in the porta-potty for a while and then you disappeared. We could have sent the extra volunteers home and told them to come back tomorrow, but I chose to put them to work. If you don't like the decision, fire me."

Tracey grabbed her hard hat and walked past her cousin, going toward one of the houses that had men and women working in every corner. Foremen gave instructions that were followed explicitly.

Trina watched protectively from the canopy. "She didn't have to say I was in the porta-potty. That's not cool."

"Give her a break. She's having a hard time."

Trina shrugged and Reno was reminded of Chloe. For a second, Trina seemed to be having a memory as well. Her face softened and all he could think was that there was nothing more beautiful.

He had to stop admiring her and busied himself with the strap of his tool belt instead, still unsure why he'd come. She certainly hadn't invited him. She hadn't returned his calls either. But being here wasn't just about her.

"Why did Tracey confide in you? I mean if she'd told me she was having problems with her feet, I would have taken her to the podiatrist. Maybe that explains why she's been so sad and angry."

Reno didn't comment as he signed a medical waiver and placed a Crawford Construction paperweight on top. He grabbed a hard hat and two ice-cold bottled waters and left the tent.

"Reno, I heard Tracey talking to you. Is she—"

"Why don't you ask her? If you care."

Trina grabbed his arm. They stopped walking and she let go.

"Of course I care. I just haven't had time for anything besides work. I've been working for this for a long time, Reno. I won't feel guilty for wanting success."

"Are we talking about you again, Trina, because I thought we were talking about why your cousin has been depressed for over a month and you've never talked to her about it. Why can't you open up to the people around you? What's beneath the surface? Everybody out here is real. Why aren't you?"

"I am," she whispered.

"What did my daughter say? That was the most significant thing that's happened in my life recently. My daughter talked for the first time in almost a year and you didn't explain anything to me. That was wrong."

"I told you." She wiped a tear that had escaped.

"You didn't tell me how and why it happened. I've been waiting for this day forever. She chose to talk to you, and what do you do? You walked out on me."

"Because Nona—"

"Left, a minute after you. But you didn't stick around for that either."

Trina took a deep breath. "Chloe and I were at the pond and some ducks ran over when I rattled some candy paper. I had some M&Ms in my purse and broke one in half and gave it to Chloe."

"She doesn't eat candy."

Trina wiped her forehead and looked at him. "I didn't know. Chloe frowned and then the ducks came and she climbed all over me to get away. So I covered her with my jacket and scared them off. Then I pretended I couldn't find her."

"Where was she?"

"Right next to me on the bench. I kept saying 'where's Chloe? I'm going to cry. Boo-hoo' and the more I did that, the more she peeked out. Then she popped out, and I said I was glad I found her, and could I have a hug?"

"Slow down. What did she do?" Reno guided Trina past a tree and listened with his head down.

"She hugged me."

"Chloe hugged you?" He looked off into the blue sky, a plane making white ski tracks overhead. His baby was growing into a little girl so quickly.

Trina was having a positive effect on her. But it wouldn't last. She needed a mother and a temporary one wouldn't do.

"Chloe won't touch anyone except Mrs. Teralyn or me."

"She hugged me for a long time and patted my back. Like this," she demonstrated, over his left shoulder. "We had a girl moment, and then we talked about shoes."

"What's a girl moment," he said, touching her wrist, then deciding to let it go.

"It's personal. Nothing bad. Just between us girls."

Reno decided to let them have their little secret. Trina had given him a gift. His baby had spoken for the first time in twelve months. "Was Chloe talking to you conversationally? Because that would be unusual. She sometimes spoke both English and common Somali at once."

Trina shook her head. "No. Nothing like that. She talked in her own way. Nodding or shrugging."

"I see. What else?"

"I asked her if she wanted to be my new best friend and she looked like she was thinking about it. She crossed her legs like mine, folded her hands like I fold mine. Then we made a bouquet of flowers and put some in our shoes, and I asked her if she knew the way home. She took my hand and we walked on the path to the sidewalk. We got to the curb and she pointed to your house and said, *home*."

"Are you sure?" he asked.

"I've thought about it a thousand times. She said it, Reno. She said home."

For a few seconds he couldn't find the right words. "I would have liked to have known this last week when it happened."

Reno walked a few steps processing everything he'd heard. His baby had talked. That meant she was on her way back from whatever traumatic place she'd been.

Trina's shadow shielded him. "I understand that you overheard Nona and you got the wrong impression."

"No, I didn't."

"I believe you did," Reno said.

"Trina? The drywall's been hung and we're ready for you to start taping." A man in a hard hat and blue jeans left the dirt patch that would have sod on it once the house was complete, and came over to them.

He was related to Trina, Reno could tell because of the similar coloring and eyes, but construction was his profession. His shirt also said "foreman." "Blue McKendree," he said, extending his hand. "Trina's cousin."

Reno shook it. "Reno Merriwether. Brought my tools in case you need an electrician."

"Certified?"

Reno pulled out his card and handed it over. "Yes. My certification is current."

"Excellent. We had a man get a little too much sun earlier, so we've been waiting for the union to send someone else over."

"What hall?"

"Fifty-four."

"That's mine. If he doesn't get here in a few minutes you can give them a call. I won't cut a man out of a day's pay, so I'm here if you need me."

His expression said he approved of Reno's work ethic.

"Alright," Blue said, "Let's get you started before we lose any more daylight hours."

"Blue?" Another man called as he emerged from between the two houses. "Can we get you back here for a minute? We have a spacing problem with the refrigerator."

"The appliances shouldn't be here yet," Blue said.

"I know. Can you step back here for a minute?"

Blue shook Reno's hand and chucked Trina under her chin. "Be right back," he said to them and took off.

Trina took the sidewalk and Reno followed her. Men and women taped drywall and seemed happy. Everybody except Trina.

"While we have a minute, let's finish our conversation," he said, glad someone had started playing music softly in the distance.

"You were so good at male bonding, I thought you'd forgotten I was here."

"No one can forget you, Trina."

"Nona thinks so."

"Friendship is a two-way street. If she had a problem with you, she could have said something."

"Don't let me off the hook. A lot of what she said was true. I never asked about her mother, but they didn't get along. I thought I was sparing Nona's feelings, but I guess not. And I didn't know she'd had her gall bladder removed. That's something you tell your friends when you're in the ER, but that's no excuse. I should have been a better friend."

"You don't know if she was already plotting against you, Trina."

"That wasn't Nona's style. She was a nice person. We'd been best friends for a long time."

Two couples in scrubs walked past them flirting while carrying ice water. Love was in the air and Reno couldn't help but wish it was him. "What do you want to say, Trina?"

"I apologize for leaving the way I did. I was upset, unclear about how I felt about Nona being there. I didn't like what she was saying— especially since what she said was true."

He wanted to hold her now and make her smile again. In this moment he knew he loved her. Marrying someone else would be the hardest thing he would ever do in his life.

"Now you know, so move on," he suggested. She nodded but didn't look like she was going to go any easier on herself.

They had walked to the corner and stopped. Everything ahead of them was in need of revitalization. Maybe Crawford Construction would be able to rehab more houses.

A gust of wind ruffled the front of Trina's shirt.

Memories of her in his office, with eyes that said yes, teased him. She'd occupied the better part of his daily thoughts and seeing her in pain wasn't bearable.

"What are you thinking, Reno?"

He gazed at her. "That I could turn back the clock and not be a fool."

The vein in her neck pulsed. "Have you found a mother for Chloe?"

"Yes."

Her head sank to her chest and two tears squeezed past long black lashes.

He put his arm around her shoulders. "But

she's got these goals and more than anything, I want her to be happy. So I'm still looking."

She folded his T-shirt into her hands, their chests meeting. Tears streaked her cheeks. "I'm not perfect for you. I don't want you to have regrets, and I don't want to break your hearts. You need someone who is settled in their life and not searching for her place like I am," she whispered. "Don't want me, Reno."

"But I already do."

"I'm letting you down. I don't want to disappoint you after all you've done for me."

Her tears had dried and he let his hands caress her arms. "The only way I want you is fully and completely. Anything else is unsatisfactory."

Reno didn't know his body could ache from wanting someone. But not this way.

The swell and echo of hammers grew louder as they walked closer to the house. She watched a car go by. "What's Drake doing here?"

He bumped the Mercedes CLK onto the curb and got out. Weaving slightly he jogged across the street, headed straight for Trina. "I need to talk to you."

Reno eyed Drake speculatively, then turned to Trina. "Do you want to talk to him?"

She seemed to gauge Drake, then looked back at the groups of men and women working. "Sure. I'll talk to him. Would you mind excusing us?"

"That means get lost," Drake added sarcastically.

"You're only standing here because she didn't say toss you out. Don't think it can't happen."

Trina's eyes were wide with surprise when

Reno looked at her. "I'll be over there with your cousins, if you need me."

"Okay." Her hands grazed both his arms and Drake didn't miss the gesture.

Angry, he walked inside a canopy with plastic flaps. Shayla, the pregnant cousin he'd heard so much about, was seated in a chair looking radiant with a man beside her. She looked so much like Trina it was startling.

"I'm Reno Merriwether. A friend of Trina's," he said and offered his hand.

The man stood and shook. "Jake Parker. This is my wife, Shayla Crawford-Parker."

"We know who you are, Reno." Shayla extended well-manicured fingers to him. "Please excuse me. I need to stay seated or my husband will have a fit."

Jake took Shayla's hand and kissed it, love lingering in his eyes. "You're supposed to be taking it easy."

"I've been so sedentary, I'm moving backwards." Shayla teased him. "Reno, you're staring at me. Does my husband have a reason to get jealous?"

Embarrassed, he looked away, then back. "Forgive me, but you're gorgeous. No disrespect intended," he said quickly to Jake. He forced himself to look away.

"Don't be shy," Shayla said. "You can look at me as much as you want."

Laughter burst out of him. Jake rubbed her thigh. "Honey, you're embarrassing him."

The ice was broken. Reno relaxed. "You all resemble each other so closely, it's uncanny."

"We've heard that a lot. My cousin told me a lot about you, but she's close-mouthed about the juicy details."

"On that note, I'm going to get a sub. Reno, can I bring you one?" Jake asked.

He still remembered his egg white and wheat toast breakfast before his morning run. "No, it's only ten-thirty."

"And what's that supposed to mean?" Imperial eyebrows arched his way.

"Nothing, ma'am. Nothing at all." Reno nodded, knowing his place.

"Be back in ten minutes," Shayla said and winked at Jake. "Be nice."

"That's no fun."

Reno enjoyed the banter between the couple. He craved a relationship like theirs almost as much as Shayla craved food. But he had to get over this thing for Trina.

"Do you need a hand?" he asked Jake. "I might be better off going with you."

"No thanks, man. Welcome to Crawford's Island. Incoming." Jake was referring to Tracey, Trisha, and two other cousins that looked like Shayla. But before they could converge upon the canopy, they were sidetracked by men.

"Shayla and I are doctors," Jake explained to Reno and handed him a two-way radio. "If anyone needs medical help, she can only dial an ambulance. There are two other doctors and nurses on the premises. Press this button, and they'll come running."

"Sweetheart, don't forget to bring me some chips," Shayla called.

Jake winked and Reno could feel the current of love between them.

Reno took Jake's seat. "You two have something that's extraordinary. I'm envious."

Shayla's gaze softened. "We've been married four years and we worked our way up from that heated passionate love to a respectful love, to tender love."

Reno leaned forward, drawn in by her calm aura.

Shayla couldn't have been much older than he was, but she seemed wise for her years.

"I was married for eight years and I don't believe we ever had any love except the first one," Reno confessed. "Then disappointment set in when we found out we couldn't have a baby, and that consumed our relationship."

"Jake and I have a special something else, Reno."

"What is it?"

"Binding love."

Could he have done more to save his relationship with Dana? Six months before the relationship completely ended, he'd wanted to give up, but he'd stayed because of Chloe. He thought he'd known every form of love there was, but he found himself wondering what Shayla knew that he didn't.

He wondered if he had all that was necessary to enter into a healthy relationship with any woman, including Trina. He knew he loved her. But binding love? "What does it feel like?"

"We've bonded and learned each other's quirks, likes, and dislikes. Moods, temperament, joys, fears, and passions. He loves and accepts every part of me, and I love and accept every part of him. We forgive each other and we laugh a lot. I won't hurt him, not even a little bit. And if I do, I make it better. He feels the same about me."

Thunder rumbled, but nobody stopped working.

The second beautiful breeze of the day caressed the flaps of the canopy in a wave, like the tide rolling into the beach and then retreating. Everyone arched into the wind that coated them in coolness before it moved on.

"Do you hear them?" she asked. "They're all saying the same thing. That was beautiful." Shayla caressed her belly. "Did you ever feel that you accepted every part of your wife?" Shayla pulled out of a bag a thinly sliced Granny Smith apple. She offered him a piece and he accepted.

"No." The word popped out. "I don't want to tear my ex-wife down. Everything that happened wasn't her fault. I thought I would love her forever, but when she got angry because we couldn't conceive, I didn't know how to handle it. A baby was so important to her, and I didn't realize how much love she'd lost for me by not having one. My life has been forever changed by Chloe, our, well, my four-year-old daughter."

Jake walked back in with the subs, pushing the flaps open so they could have an unobstructed view.

"That was quick," Reno said.

"They were down the street. My wife must have made it sound urgent."

Reno laughed. "She's a pistol."

"I'm glad you see what I'm working with."

Shayla took the chips from Jake, and set the apples on the tray. "Your daughter's adopted?"

"Yes, from Somalia. She's my heart. We're all each other's got, for now."

"What do you mean?" Shayla ate, then took the napkin from her husband's open hand to wipe her mouth.

Jake caressed her shoulder and she unconsciously rubbed his knee.

"My daughter has a sister, and I have the opportunity to adopt her, too."

Jake's brow creased. "I read something online about Somalian adoptions. You have to do it before April first, because after that they'll stop foreign adoptions for the remainder of the year so they can review their policies. Something to that effect."

"That's right," Reno said.

"Shayla," Tracey called. "Trina's getting ready to speak."

Reno stood up with her cousins. Trina walked to the front of the houses and accepted the bullhorn from her brother. She tested it and it squeaked, sending hands to ears. Everyone laughed, then clapped for her.

Trina bowed, but when she realized they were giving her an ovation, she covered her eyes and put her head on her brother's shoulder. Reno watched her from the front of the medical tent, but could hear the "damn she's fine," ten men back.

He wasn't the only one who appreciated her charm, intelligence, and beauty.

But he was the only one who'd committed his heart to her.

"Thank you so much," Trina said. "For showing up!" Everyone laughed. "No, really. For building houses to help someone less fortunate than you. To committing a day to being good to someone else. To working together. We're connecting with the community," she said. "We're connecting with each other, I hope," she said, and the crowd roared. "This effort is about doing for others, but it's also about doing for ourselves, so be good to each other. Have fun, be safe, and please don't leave before I've had a chance to say *hello*. Thank you!"

"I'll see you later." he said to Shayla and Jake who waved, eating their subs.

Leaving the tent, Reno grabbed an ice water and skimmed the wetness off the bottle with his hand. Moving around the circle of people, he loosened the top and handed it to Trina who needed it after a half hour of talking.

"You want some?" she asked, tilting the half-empty bottle at him.

"Trina, can we get you two up here on the second floor to wash off these windows?" her cousin called from the window.

"Sure." Reno let Trina go up the stairs ahead of him. The room was small with the wall freshly painted eggshell.

"Towel, spray. The windows fold in like this." Blue demonstrated. "Have fun."

He slapped Reno on the back. "Keep an eye on her. She's a wanderer."

"Blue, you're going to get beat up like that time in second grade."

He gave Trina a playful shove. "You were a foot taller than me and I had an eye patch."

Trina started laughing. "I'd forgotten about that."

"She'll exploit your handicap, man. You gotta watch her."

"Don't worry, man. I can't watch anything else."

They started cleaning the windows, the air in the room hot and still.

"Hot?" he asked her.

Trina set down the spray and peeled off her T-shirt, leaving a pink camisole. "I can't believe they don't have the air conditioning going."

"It'd just be cooling the outside."

They wiped down the windows, windowsills, doorknobs, and fixtures, then picked up the supplies and moved to the next room.

Perspiring, Reno used his shirt to mop his brow. He opened the stepladder so Trina could wipe off the globes. He had a bird's-eye view of her stomach, and all he wanted to do was kiss skin so brown and smooth, it reminded him of the Sahara desert.

Inadvertently his chin grazed her stomach and she shook a bit. Reno held her waist, steadying her.

He enjoyed the effect he was having on her.

"I gave Chloe my lip gloss. At first I didn't think she'd take it, but she did."

"Love Nectar," he said, his mouth inches from hers.

"I was going to ask how you knew, but you'd

remember something like that. You're Reno Merriwether."

"Come here," he said in her ear.

Trina turned just enough. "What? What do you want with me?" she said, almost sobbing.

"I want to kiss you."

"Here?" she asked. "I'm sweaty and dirty and—"

"Now," he said, "right now." He didn't look into her eyes. "I don't want you to think anymore."

"Yes—"

His lips touched hers and every part of him sang. Like rain to an ocean, she filled him.

The kiss deepened and he savored her tongue and her desire. He pulled back a little, but she leaned into him. Nothing else mattered. Not heat or salty sweat. Not past sins or painful slights. He wanted her and she wanted him. His lips slid from hers and went down her chin and neck.

They were in public, he reminded himself. He opened his eyes and saw Trina's ex-boyfriend Drake.

"Drake is still here," he said in her ear.

"I don't care." Trina rested her head against his chest. "Maybe he wants to join Suddenly-singleatl.com and find a date."

"He's asking around and everyone is pointing to this house. We'd better meet him downstairs."

"He's ruining the best part of my day."

"Don't let him ruin anything. I'd like for this to continue. Would you?"

Trina nodded.

"Come back to my place," he said.

"What about Chloe and your babysitter?"

"Mrs. Teralyn has seven children. I don't think she needs lessons in the art of making love."

"Probably not." She looked up at him, and a part of himself that he'd held in reserve gave way under her smoky gaze. "Making love sounds so sexy coming from your mouth."

"It feels sexy, too. But before I sweep you off your feet, you have to make him go away."

Trina pressed her lips to Reno's chin, then walked down the stairs and out the house.

Drake's impatience was immediate when he saw them.

"He looks terrible," Trina said, and nervously scratched Reno's palm.

He caressed the bare part of her back. "He looks like he's been drinking even more since you last talked to him. Are you sure you even want to talk to him?"

"Yeah, but not in private. We really don't have anything more to say to each other."

"Then it should be short and sweet." Reno hated that jealousy was able to stamp out the desire he'd felt for Trina seconds ago.

"Nothing ever is with him." Trina walked over to Drake and pointed him to the same tree he'd taken Trina down an hour ago.

Reno couldn't hear their conversation at first, but it was quickly escalating. They'd moved between two cars, their conversation absorbed in the noise of hammers and saws.

Reno moved closer, making sure he stayed within range in case Trina needed him. "Drake, you sold me out to Nona. Why should I help you?"

"I was on the rebound ever since you broke up

with me. I wasn't in my right mind. I know I was wrong, but you should give me the benefit of the doubt."

At the corner of the second house, Tippy Hudson and his camera crew had set up and were interviewing Trina's helpers who were happy to talk about their love connections.

He looked inside the canopy and Jake and Shayla were gone, their food and water abandoned.

Drake was getting louder and Trina kept shaking her head. She looked as if she were getting more upset and she started glancing around as if looking for help.

If Tippy got wind that Drake was there, he'd turn this event into a circus and all of Trina's effort to set herself apart would go down the drain.

Reno walked over and touched Trina's arm. She turned into him, the movement intimate.

"You've got more company. Tippy's here," he said in her ear.

Trust flickered in her eyes, but she looked tired and undecided. Nothing would have given Reno more pleasure than making her troubles go away by putting her to sleep in his bed.

Like an overgrown child, Drake tried to shove his way between them and grew angrier when he couldn't.

Trina had linked her fingers with Reno's and he kissed them.

"We're in the middle of something." The heady odor of scotch on Drake's breath made Reno understand what had given him false courage.

"Don't make the mistake of thinking I won't drop you right here," Reno told him.

"Do you know who I am? I'm her fiancé."

"You sure about that?" Reno said. "Even I heard her say no."

"Oh, come on." Trina sounded exasperated. "Drake, just leave. I won't ask my brother to consider your firm."

Drake pretended to laugh. "Who do you think you're talking to? I could buy and sell you like that." He snapped his finger in Reno's face.

"Trina, it's time to leave," Reno said. "Before this gets out of hand."

"She's not going anywhere. She embarrassed me in front of the nation. My business has suffered because of your mouth," he said to Trina. "You owe me this one favor. Now tell your hired boy here to take a hike and we can get this deal done."

"I agree, Reno," she said softly. "It's time to leave."

"You're not going anywhere until we settle how you're going to make this up to me," Drake spat.

Drake grabbed Trina's shoulder and pulled. She stumbled, and grasped her shirt. Reno grabbed Drake's hand and twisted it behind his back until the man was on his knees.

Drake screamed and the camera filmed.

"Nicely done," said a tall, muscular man who looked like a Crawford. "I'll take the trash out. I'm Nick Crawford. Trina's uncle."

Trina huddled close to her uncle, having not once looked at Reno. He wanted to take her hand, but the crowd prevented him from saying anything. He noticed Tippy had gotten a clear shot of everything from the street. He did a mock salute with his microphone and hurried away.

"Uncle Nick, please. Make this go away. He tore my top."

Though casually dressed, Nick was no less military.

One of the ladies handed Reno a T-shirt for Trina. "Thank you." She didn't even look at him. Reno knew where this was going.

"Shayla went to the hospital. She's having the baby," Tracey said quietly. "They didn't want to disturb you."

Nick grabbed Drake by his forearm, bringing him up to his feet. He stumbled, making it obvious to all that he was under the influence.

Reno opened the T-shirt for Trina, her hands were shaking so bad. She pulled it down over her head, jabbed her arms through, then hurried to stand with Blue.

"Do you need him for anything else?" Nick asked.

"No, Unc. Please get him out of here, and I don't ever want to see him again. Reno? Please, go with them."

He wasn't even shocked. Grabbing his tools, he walked off in the opposite direction, knowing it was time to give up hope for Trina forever.

Chapter 12

The tiny wail of the baby distracted Trina as she flipped the channels between Fox 5 news, 11Alive, and WSB-TV. Yesterday had been a slow news day with no cop shootings, no tornado alerts, and no ATM smashes and grabs; so, they'd run the clip of the construction site, too many times for comfort.

Yesterday she'd given up on television and had started listening to the radio. But the most popular stations in Atlanta had found a good reason to talk about the Crawford family, and they lived it up.

In a show of media rebellion, she'd turned to her iPod and enjoyed the soothing croon of Joe Sample and Lalah Hathaway, yet she was far from settled. She hadn't slept and she couldn't stay focused at work.

She'd given up and had battled lunch-hour traffic early this afternoon to visit Shayla at her parents' exclusive Gales Hillside Subdivision.

Shayla lounged in the massive sunroom filled

with overflowing pillowed couches decorated in warm colors of burnt reds, brown, orange, and yellow.

The outside world ceased to matter every other time Trina had come into this room, but today she was filled with anxiety.

"Why hasn't a celebrity driven into a tree?" she said to Shayla, who nursed her daughter, Sienna.

"Is that nice?" Shayla sounded so tranquil, Trina was envious.

This was the same woman who said she'd tried to scream the paint off the birthing room walls, according to Tracey's report. Who'd confessed to squeezing the nurse's hand so hard she thought she'd broken a bone. The one who'd demanded an immediate divorce if her husband ever impregnated her again. Shayla, who had recounted in horrifying detail the hours of her labor and delivery. Now she was so serene Trina wanted to shake the old trash-talking Shayla out.

Trina ignored the plate of fresh fruit Maria, the house manager, had put in front of them. "I don't like your current, 'I'm so happy' attitude, and I can't wait for the real you to come back."

"I have a baby now, and she makes me feel calm. She's quiet, so I'm quiet."

"Where's your husband? I'm sure he's going to want the real you back?"

"There was a small fire at our office in Mississippi, so he and Daddy went to check it out."

"Anything serious?"

"No. The fire department chief urged them to come back for the day. Mom's at the hairdresser and Scooter is at school, no doubt in somebody's time-out chair. So it's me and Sienna holding down the homefront. And now you, with all your negative energy. Have you talked to Reno?"

"No, but this isn't about him."

"What isn't?"

"This conversation." Anger made her voice sound louder. Sienna's little arm shot into the air.

"I'm sorry. But I'm frustrated."

"What's wrong, honey?"

"I'm tired of being the butt of everyone's joke. I can't listen to the radio without having to hear what happened at the Next Step project. Apparently, it's a hot topic."

"Have you tried looking at it another way?"

"What other way? The radio jocks enjoy my embarrassment. I want to be left alone to run my business."

"Your business is people."

"The things they talk about aren't positive. They keep harping on the fact that Drake tore my top. Someone took pictures of Reno helping me put on the T-shirt."

"You're lucky, Trina, and you don't even know it."

The tiny beauty smiled in her sleep and Trina remembered how good it felt to hold Sienna the first time. Her heart had swelled with a gentle love, the same love she had experienced with Chloe.

Why was it when nothing in her life made sense, she could experience such peacefulness with a child who didn't talk?

She hadn't wanted to be anywhere else when she was with Chloe.

Acknowledging her true feelings lessened her

stress, but an undercurrent of anxiety prevented true tranquility.

Trina loved her job and she wasn't going to give it up. She didn't consider it lucky only to grab unwanted attention.

"How am I lucky?" What was Shayla's logic? "That Nick didn't have Drake tossed in jail for trespassing?"

Shayla kissed Sienna. "Make things right with Reno. From what I heard from Deion, Reno had Drake on his knees. He was protecting you."

The whole scene replayed in Trina's mind. "Drake tried to dismiss Reno as a hired hand. Reno didn't do anything, but when Drake put his hands on me, that was it."

"That's no less than I'd expect from any man in our family. Have you apologized?"

Trina couldn't bring herself to answer.

"Trina, you're not being honest, and if you make me tell you everything, you won't learn what you're doing wrong. That was the most difficult lesson I had to learn when I moved to Mississippi."

A protest built on Trina's lips, but Sienna's stretching made her pause. She hated self-examination because it always required change.

Sitting here in this peaceful place was what she wanted, but she didn't want to give up her life to have it.

"If you're a hundred percent pleased with everything you've done, give yourself a break and use the momentum for the next event."

"I haven't called him. I asked him to leave the

construction site," she finally confessed, taking comfort in unburdening herself. "He was only trying to help me and I was embarrassed. A second after I said it, I wanted to take the words back. I wanted to erase the situation. I wanted them both gone."

"That could be why you're still so bothered. Why didn't you tell him the truth?"

"I don't know. I wanted everybody there to forget about Drake and his ridiculous behavior. And if Reno had stayed, that would have been all people talked about."

"You underestimate your clients. You haven't seen your website, have you?"

"No. What now?"

"That's all they're talking about. How classy you are. How your events help people. About the love connections they give you credit for. You practice what you preach. They were glad you didn't leave the site until the last person had pulled away."

Trina rested her knuckles on her cheek. "Reno's been nothing but nice to me. He's given me advice and been my quasi–security guard. And my mentor."

"And more," Shayla said, seemingly more wise even now, two days after she had the baby.

"What more?" Trina got up and walked the length of the room, her eyes burning from long hours of work and no sleep. Long hours of her refusing to cry because she'd done Reno wrong.

Everywhere she looked was a museum of photos of her Uncle Eric and Aunt Lauren kissing, hugging, and laughing on all seven continents. Who wouldn't want that?

"It's probably too late." Trina hoped Shayla would contradict her. When her cousin said nothing, she tried to keep her misery at bay. "I just need to work harder for good publicity, right?"

"Do you know how much Nona would pay to get your kind of publicity? Especially since her carnival last night did not go well."

"How do you know that," Trina asked.

"Tracey and Trisha met some guys at your reception at the High Museum and sent them over to spy on Nona's event."

"They did it?"

"Honey, you don't know how beautiful your cousins are. I was told the rides that had been ordered were wrong. They were kid-size, and people were angry. A big man started complaining, so Nona thought plying him with drinks would quiet him down. He got louder."

Trina covered her mouth, glad that hadn't been her. "You're kidding," she whispered. "Girl, a carnival?"

"Honey, when I was thirteen, I thought Six Flags was the best place in the whole world. I couldn't go but once a year because we didn't have a lot of money. When the school gave out tickets as prizes for the top students, I made sure I won."

"Wow, you were desperate."

"Honey, I wasn't a Crawford then. I was a Webster and we had to work for everything."

Trina admired Shayla because she wasn't a spoiled brat anymore. She'd become a woman of two worlds who'd come into her own. "You really are amazing, in case you didn't know."

"Oh, I know," Shayla said, being her old sassy self. "Let me finish telling you about Miss Nona. According to Trisha's sources, when people saw that the rides were for kids, they demanded their money back. Some just left."

"What did Nona do?"

Sienna took in a shuddery breath and they both hesitated, watching to see if she was waking up. Every instinct in Trina's body said hold her, but Trina didn't, as if touching the child meant she'd have to trade the board room for the nursery.

"She's going to be asleep a while longer," Shayla said. "Nona started throwing people out, and when Brett from Fox 5 arrived to ask her the instant win question, she had her security people escort him off the fairgrounds without talking to him."

"I didn't know that! Why wasn't that on the news? I've been watching for three days."

"You cut off the TV and you stopped answering your phone."

Fishing inside her purse, Trina came up with her cell phone and dialed. "Excuse me for a minute, Shayla. Tracey?"

"Yes?"

"It's me, Trina."

"You finally decided to join the living. Where are you?"

"At Uncle Eric's with Shayla and Sienna."

"Nice vacation. When are you planning on coming back to work?"

"Today, Tracey. First, I want to apologize for

taking you for granted." Trina could see the surprise on Shayla's face. "How's it going?"

Tracey didn't say anything for a full minute, and while Trina's first instinct was to blow through the silence with words, she'd learned a lot from Chloe.

"I'm hanging in there," she said softly. "I've been seeing someone. A counselor. I've been sad for a long time so I'm glad to have someone to talk to. I've sworn off dating and even took my profile off the site."

"Tracey, don't do that. There's someone out there for you. For all of us."

"You've found your Prince Charming. But I'm working on me now." Although she sounded wounded, she didn't sound beaten down.

"Well, I'm glad you're getting the help you need. If you need some time off—"

"Trina, don't trip. I'm just seeing a counselor. So let's get back to business."

"All right." The last thing she wanted was to cause any additional stress on her cousin, so Trina let it go. "Anything new going on?"

"I already told you this, but you can't go MIA. It's hard enough trying to run the business, but when you come back and challenge decisions, it's undermining to me and the others."

"Noted. I'm sorry."

"I mean, I know it's your company, but we do work here and run it, too. Okay?"

Trina nodded, accepting the reprimand. "I'm sorry, it won't happen again. The radio stations were driving me crazy, but that doesn't give me the right to shut everybody out."

"You probably realized that after you asked Reno to leave we lost a few subscribers."

Trina felt the shame all over her body. "I figured as much. I guessed about ten. Were there more?"

"No. Ten exactly. Eight women and two men."

"I'll write personal notes and invite them back. Maybe they'll give us another shot."

"That's a good idea," Tracey said brightly.

"I'm going to put Sienna in the bed," Shayla whispered.

Trina nodded. "Tracey, anything else?"

"No. I've dealt with all the messages. The final ceremony will be April 30, and I've already confirmed our table. There were some interview requests, but I took care of those, too."

"Excellent work, girl. Where's Trisha?"

"On a lunch date."

"Oh, Tracey." She had good reason to be depressed with everyone dating, except her.

"Trina, stop it right there. First of all, he's nothing to write home about. But I want to add, I'm fine where I am. I don't want to get into a relationship dragging around baggage from the past. So, good luck to Trisha. Her guy wants me to hook up with his cousin, but no thanks. His name is Beetle, and he has a ridiculous laugh."

Trina giggled.

"No way," Tracey said, laughing.

"Sounds like you're using good judgment on this one."

"I am. Anything else," Tracey asked.

"Has Reno called?" Trina asked finally.

"Yes. He was really nice to me at the construction site."

"I overheard you two talking and when I asked him what about, he said to talk to you."

"That's very cool. I can't believe he kept my secret. I like him."

Trina pressed her lips together. "Cool wasn't what I was thinking at the time."

"He's a nice man. Give him a call. Gotta go. Bye."

Tracey hung up, and Trina ate some fruit.

"Sienna's sound asleep," Shayla said when she walked back into the room. She climbed on the couch, tossing a chenille throw over her legs. "I think I'll nap, too."

"Of course. I'm so dense." Trina touched her forehead. Had she taken care of business days ago, she wouldn't be here now exhausting her cousin and her newborn. "I'll call you in a couple days."

"Trina, you don't have to leave this second. You look like you could use a nap, too."

Trina hugged her cousin. "A nap sounds wonderful, but I have to get something settled with Reno before I fall asleep tonight."

Shayla walked her to the front door and pulled it open. "I hope you two work it out."

Trina kept her hopes to herself. Especially because they changed hourly. "We'll talk soon."

Driving up Highway 141, Trina dialed Reno and got his voice mail. "Reno, it's me, Trina. I-I wanted to come by and talk to you. You're out so, well, thank you for everything you did at the Next Step Project. I wanted to apologize, but in person. And I wanted to finish the discussion we started. When you get a chance, please call me on my cell."

She hung up and merged into traffic on I-285 that wrapped around Atlanta and found herself in an inadvertent parking lot. Tuning into 750 AM, she waited for the traffic report.

A two-car accident was a mile ahead, and she was hours from home. Taking Ashford Dunwoody Road, she parked at the Perimeter Mall.

Maybe a nice trinket would settle the disquiet she felt.

Victoria's Secret beckoned, and Trina answered with a white satin nightie, pink silk boy shorts and a bra, and a black fishnet body suit.

Stopping at the MAC store, she replaced the lip gloss she'd given to Chloe and felt that glowing warmth again. Maybe Chloe would like a toy. Trina headed for Dillard's and selected two stuffed bears and a dress.

Pulling out her credit card to pay, Trina eyed the remaining identical dress. Reno would have both girls soon. She grabbed the other one and got back in line. Paying, she was signing her name when her BlackBerry vibrated.

Come over tonight after nine. R.

Relief raced up her body.

Tonight was the night. Trina knew she'd have to commit or walk away.

Chapter 13

The tickets to Somalia weighed heavily in Reno's hand, almost as heavy as the decision he'd made to leave Trina alone.

Putting them back into the safe, he closed the door, the electronic mechanisms automatically locking the contents.

Tonight he was a man with few remaining options.

He'd proposed to three women today, and so far, nobody had called him back.

He was stressed out.

Walking through the dark house, he could hardly find comfort in the hard work he'd put into refinishing the floors the first three months after Dana had left. Or the royal mess he'd made painstakingly painting every wall in the house in month four, paying to have the house professionally repainted in month five, or the furniture he'd spent restless nights choosing online just more than a month ago.

All of his anger and frustration, disappointment,

and determination had gone into installing the outdoor privacy fence and laying the stones on the patio.

For all intents and purposes, his home was aesthetically complete.

But comfort found no resting place in him.

The day was about over, and no Trina.

Uncapping his second Heineken, he took it along with his favorite blanket out on the patio and sat in front of the house's best feature, the outdoor fireplace.

He was glad he sacrificed his 401k and had bought out Dana's half of the house. He had made the money back, and his soul was at rest here because this was the perfect home for a family.

Orange and blue flames played with the darkness, and he sat down on the canopied swing for two, gazing at the stars, wondering what his other daughter was doing half a world away.

Chloe had been asleep for about thirty minutes, and Reno was glad. Her refusal to speak to him had been this week's second greatest disappointment. He picked up the baby monitor and listened to her breathe, glad she was alive, glad she was his, even if at four he couldn't understand her.

She'd spoken to Trina though, and despite being a mature man, he was jealous.

He gently set the monitor down and walked around the deck to settle his restless nerves, but found himself back at the chair, shaking out his blanket, and knocking over his beer.

He swallowed a curse, not wanting to resume the bad habit.

Snatching up the bottle, he headed to the kitchen for paper towels and was back on the deck mopping up the spill when the doorbell rang.

Not wanting the doorbell to awaken Chloe, he pulled the front door open.

Trina looked as beautiful as he'd ever seen her, and scared, too.

"Hi," she said. "May I come in?"

He couldn't act as if everything was okay between them. He wasn't even sure why she'd come here. He'd keep things short and sweet and mentally move forward with his life and new wife. Whoever she was.

He gestured her in.

Going back on the deck, he finished cleaning up the mess and tossed the towels into the small garbage can beside the grill. Sitting down on the swing, he swallowed the remaining beer.

Silently she watched him from inside the sliding screen door.

"Close the door or the house will fill up with bugs."

She stepped onto the patio and slid the screen in place.

He turned his attention to the sky and located the star of Venus.

"Reno, will you look at me?"

"No."

Her high heels crunched on the inlaid stones and it took iron man strength not to look at her. He loved her feet.

Instead of sitting, she stood in front of him and stopped the swing with her leg.

"I want to apologize for my behavior at the

Next Step Project. It was unfair, and I shouldn't have asked you to leave. I'm sorry."

"Thanks. Goodnight."

"I'm not leaving. I let you go when we were at Georgia, and I'm not going to let that happen again. I know how it looked, and it was wrong." She held onto the swing, slowing the rocking motion.

"Trina, how it looked isn't important to me. You lumped me in with your ex and dismissed me. That showed me that I meant nothing to you. You're days away from getting everything you've ever wanted. Congratulations, in advance. Now if you don't mind, I've got things to do."

"Reno," she pleaded. "I know that I've hurt you and I'm sorry," she added, her voice catching on tears. "I was wrong. I was so stressed out. But that's no excuse for being selfish and ungrateful. You've helped me build my company and I wish you would say you forgive me."

She reached for his face.

"Don't, Trina. Don't!" He held her hands, his resolve drifting away with every plea. But she wasn't for him. She'd proven that.

"I have to let you go. What happened out there was the final straw. I asked you to be my wife so I can get my daughter. When you said no the first time, I should have walked away then. I'm walking now."

"I wanted to talk to you about that."

He looked up, seeing her trim belted waist, then her cleavage. The smooth columns of her neck beckoned him and then the determined tilt to her jaw.

"Don't play games with me."

"Forgive me first."

"Why you first again? Should I have believed Nona? You're not tapped in to what other people need or want from you."

She nodded, although tears ran down her cheeks. "I am, Reno. That's why I'm here trying to make up with you."

Making up implied there was a relationship. He held his position, not wanting to have hope where there was none. He still wanted her. With all his heart.

Trina reached for him and this time he didn't have the strength to push her away. "Sweetheart, we can get past this."

He shook his head. "I forgive you, okay? Now please leave."

Trina wrapped her arms around his neck, her cheek on top of his head. She pressed kisses on his head, eyes, and lips. Enveloped by her sensualness, and her repeated whispered apologies, he searched within himself for the strength to push her away. Digging deep, he set her back a step and tried to stand.

"Unwrap me," she urged, her hands caressing his neck.

"What?"

"I'm your make up gift." She let him go long enough to pull the belt ends from her pocket and put them in his hands.

"Aren't wrapped presents the best kind?"

"Trina, I can't want you anymore." He'd only had two beers. He wasn't that drunk. She didn't stop pressing gentle kisses into his face and neck. "What are you doing?"

"Seducing you," she said.

Reno remembered every time he'd played the lottery. He could still recall every traffic ticket he'd almost beat and every contest he didn't win.

He'd hit the jackpot, but he wasn't sure if the prize was going to cost him too much.

Hooking his fingers through the belt loops, he unwound it and the coat fell open. There was nothing but Trina and pretty pink briefs and a tiny pink bra.

"Why?" He had to know. He was about to dive head first into the darkest part of the ocean with a woman who hadn't given him a single reason to trust her.

"Why what?" She straightened her arms and the coat slipped to the ground. It wasn't until the coat pooled around her feet that he noticed his favorite crystal shoes accentuated by pink toes. Hot damn!

Reno thanked his lucky stars he had a privacy fence.

He sat back and looked up at her. The question as to why she was seducing him still rattled around in his brain, but his second head was in control of his body, and Reno gave way to its power.

"Why are you seducing me?"

"Because I want you."

The weight of each word signaled the turn he'd been wanting from that first meeting at Intermezzo.

"Do you know what you're doing?" he asked, his hands roaming her back, butt and thighs. "And I mean really know, because I can't go another round with you, Trina. You know what I want. Can you give it to me?"

"You want me," she stated, her gaze never leaving his.

"You know that I do."

His cell phone vibrated in his pocket, breaking up her seduction plan. He'd given the three potential wives his private number.

Reno ignored the vibration and focused on the woman of his dreams.

"Can we go inside?" Trina asked.

The phone vibrated and hummed again and reality pressed in. He couldn't ignore the call he'd been waiting for.

Her gaze was fixed on him.

"I have to take this." He pulled the phone from his pocket and looked at the screen. "She was my second choice."

Trina touched his hand. "Was I your first?"

"You know you are."

He pressed the button.

"I'd like to be your wife."

The words came at the same time from both women and Reno did the only thing he could. "I found someone already. Thank you," he said.

Tears poured from Trina's eyes. "I'm too late again. Reno, I'm sorry." She started to back away. "Good luck to you and the girls."

She picked up her coat and got her arm through the sleeve.

Slowly he set the phone on the swing face down. "Mrs. Merriwether to be, can I have a kiss?"

Trina looked over her shoulder as if another woman had materialized out of thin air.

"I'm talking to you, Trina Crawford. Can I have a kiss?"

The coat slipped from her hands and she embraced him.

A sob rolled up from her chest.

"I won't kiss you, if you're crying."

"You're going to miss a lot of kisses. I cry. A lot."

"Not now, baby. This is something to celebrate."

"That's what I was hoping for."

"If you're sure . . ."

For a second, she looked sorry that he needed reassurance, but Reno didn't want to misunderstand a thing.

Her tender lips met his and though wanting her physically had been on his mind for weeks, he had to know for sure.

"I'm sure I want to make love to you," she said, and Reno believed her. "And I'm sure I want to be your wife."

He'd heard all he needed to. "Let's go inside," he offered, the mosquitoes out in force.

She reached behind her back and unsnapped her bra, letting it fall. Then she stepped out of her panties. "Why?"

From top to bottom she was smooth except for her glittering shoes. And they were just too sexy to take off.

"You were never more beautiful."

He slowly pulled off his top and sweatpants, leaving him as bare as she was.

"I could say the same."

Taking her in his arms, he kissed her with all the pent up passion he controlled for months. This was their night and though he didn't know how long it would last, he was glad for the time right now. Taking her to the lounge chair, he followed her down and kissed every inch of her body, concentrating on her curves and grooves.

"What are you hoping to get from our marriage?" he asked, his fingers playing in the softness between her legs. Her breathing was ragged, her body sensitive and responsive to his every touch.

"I want to help you and Chloe and Christina. I want to help make your family whole."

Her words healed spaces long deserted by divorce, and the loss of his daughter's mother. He'd wanted Trina there so badly, had fantasized about this every night since he'd seen her on television weeks ago. This was like a dream come true.

Pulling the blanket from the swing, he tossed it against the lounge chair and guided Trina down, catching the fullness of her nipple between his lips. She curled into him, her hands caressing his face, drawing him closer. Her breasts were perfect, and he loved how their smoothness glided against his tongue. Claiming her was his ultimate joy and he wanted to savor every second of being with her.

Sliding his hand up her leg to her bottom, he guided her leg around his back, coaxing her to lie down as he trailed kisses over her stomach to her hip.

Pulling her foot up, he unfastened the first shoe, kissing her heel and her arch until he captured each toe and gently sucked.

Trina laughed. "Give me those," she said.

"They're mine now," he laughed, taking extra care with the second shoe as he had with the first.

This time he didn't stop with her toes, but kissed and caressed his way up her legs to the sensitive inside of her knees, making her plead with him to take her.

Urgently she ran her hands through his hair, and when his mouth touched the center of her sex, she braced her hands on the armrests and came off the chair in a climax that made the dogs down the street bark, and Reno proud.

He couldn't stop himself from gathering her in his arms and carrying her to his bed where he left her for a few seconds to get her shoes and coat.

When he walked back into his room he saw that she'd found the remote and had raised the lights enough to cast the room in an amber glow. He kneeled in the center of the bed and brushed her dark curls over her shoulder, replacing them with his mouth.

"Where'd the blankets go?"

"On the floor," she whispered. "Make love to me, Reno."

As far as he was concerned, he'd never received a better invitation.

Reno took Trina's ankles and pulled her to the edge of the bed. Pushing her legs up, he joined them and she cried out, reaching for him.

Their fingers locked as he moved inside her, and just the sight of how vulnerable she was almost made him come, but he held back, wanting to give her pleasure beyond her wildest imagination.

Wet heat surrounded him, and her eyes

worked a wicked magic on his heart, making him grit his teeth. She smiled at him even as her eyes grew glassy. She was going to cry, he knew. She had when they'd been in college, but they were good tears, he recalled.

"Kiss me," came the seductive command.

"No." He knew what would happen if he tasted her again. It would be all over.

"Please, Reno."

With her feet she pulled him closer, slowing his pace to a bump and grind. She arched, and her nipples taunted then invited him to sample their delicacy.

"Damn, girl," he swore, resisting.

"Tip me," she purred, sucking his fingers and then putting his thumb to work on her clitoris.

When he got it just right, her feet climbed the backs of his thighs, while her core hugged him like a glove. "That's good," she told him, flipping the script from his seduction to hers.

Her arm shot out and her abdomen tightened. If it were possible to feel more heat at the center of her wetness, he did.

Pulling hard on her thighs, he filled her, and she grabbed his wrists. "More."

Reno gave her what she asked for until he was on his toes, his sex in her to the hilt.

"Reno," she cried out against his chest, her sex quaking, tears of pleasure trickling down her face. Then he accepted his release, knowing in his heart he could never give her up.

"I want to help you and Chloe and Chritina. I want to help make your family whole."

Reno used to fantasize about making love to

her for hours, and tonight he did, until he knew the different sounds she made and why.

He loved her. Loved making love to her. And when he finally brought her to one teary climax after another, he knew this temporary arrangement had to become permanent.

Chapter 14

Trina couldn't find her panties.

She searched the floor in Reno's room and shook out all of their clothes, but they weren't mixed in. She considered going home without them, but the idea of Chloe finding them made her face burn with embarrassment.

It still looked like midnight outside, but she knew the predawn darkness was deceptive. At midnight, she'd been crying out in climax, Reno having brought her to one spiraling finish after another.

The day was about to begin, but she needed to get home to her yellow bedroom with her comfortable pillows and chaise so that she could understand why she'd let him have all of her, including the part of her heart that had never been touched by another living soul.

A delicious reminder of her last climax slid over her body as she kneeled on the floor and peered under his bed.

Reno had taken her as if their union mattered.

What was he thinking?

Deep in sleep, he snored softly, flat on his back.

Trina eyed the man she'd agreed to marry, and she couldn't help but wonder if the soft, warm, sensual, protective, happy feelings inside of her were the same kind Jake and Shayla had.

Somehow what they had seemed impossibly deeper, and Trina knew if she were going to give her heart, even temporarily, she had to have the best.

Maybe love had blinded her and that's why she couldn't find her panties.

She pulled on Reno's sweatpants, and T-shirt, covering both with her coat. Reaching down, she sought the belt, then remembered the naughty things they'd done with it. It, too, was apparently hiding with her panties.

Closing the buttons, she picked up her stilettos, knowing the two-thousand-dollar shoes were now only for the sensual enticement of her soon-to-be husband.

Closing the door to his room, her heart pounded as the meaning of the words sank in.

She was engaged to be married.

Whereas in the past the thought would have made her angry, joy now filled her heart. Trina retraced her steps to the deck and still didn't see her undergarment. Giving up, she turned and stopped short.

"Chloe!"

The little girl stood in the hallway, looking at Trina with wide eyes.

Then she smiled.

Trina's heart melted. She approached her slowly. "It's late. What are you doing up?"

Chloe shrugged and shook her head. She pointed to her father's room and pulled Trina's hand.

"Oh, no, Sweetie." Trina steered her away from the door that protected her father's nude body. "How about I tuck you back into bed?"

Chloe nodded and walked ahead of Trina, her red teddy bear pajamas so cute. They entered the little girl's fantasy room and she wanted to go and hug Reno, and assure him that Chloe and Christina would be extremely happy here.

He'd created a little girl's fantasy land with Precious Moments accessories everywhere. Chloe even had the canopied bed Trina had wanted so much as a child.

Her parents hadn't yielded to that desire, she recalled, but this was the room of her childhood dreams.

Trina took it all in and saw Chloe watching her.

"I love your room," Trina told her and Chloe nodded as if she agreed.

Trina didn't know what to do so she kneeled down and pulled back the covers. "Okay," she prompted. "Hop in."

Chloe folded her hands and looked at her.

Of course. She was waiting to say her prayers.

Chloe laid her face on her hands, and Trina knelt down, trying to remember the short version of a prayer. "*Jesus wept.*"

Chloe just looked at her.

"Sorry. That's a Bible verse. Let's see. Okay. I know. *Yea though I walk through the Valley*—"

Chloe shook her head, letting Trina know that was wrong too.

"Right. That's part of the Twenty-third Psalm. You could help me, you know."

Chloe laid her face on her hands.

Trina leaned close to hear her. Then she poked Chloe in the side. "Pss, pss, pss, pss isn't a prayer, you little cheat."

Chloe giggled aloud.

Trina stroked her back. "You have such a beautiful laugh. Tomorrow you have to laugh for Daddy, okay?"

Chloe shrugged.

"Okay, under the covers. Let's be serious. We're talking to God. Now—"

Chloe nodded vigorously, her eyes bright.

"Now is the first word?" Excited, Trina clapped. "What's the next word?"

Chloe touched her nose.

"Now nose? What kind of prayer is that?" Trina tickled Chloe's cheeks.

Another bubble of giggles burst from her. "You're the best giggler in the whole world. Okay, back to the prayer. Now what, Chloe? I'm getting sleepy fooling with you."

Chloe touched her eye.

"Now I. Oh," Trina said, remembering. "I know this, you little angel. Fold your hands."

Chloe covered her face and Trina peeked under her fingers. "Hold your hands like this. Like a steeple." When Chloe copied her, she touched her soft hair, wanting to make this child whole again. She wouldn't cry, she told herself, even as tears burned her eyes.

"You are the smartest four-year-old I've ever met. One day when you start talking again, you're going to say, 'Hi, Trina, it's me, Chloe' and I'm going to say, 'Chloe, it's great to hear your voice.'" Tears pressed at the back of her lids and she folded her hands and took a deep breath.

"Okay, let's talk to God. *Now I lay me down to sleep . . .*"

Chloe was fast asleep by the time Trina finished the prayer. She sat on the bed remembering all the childish words she'd said to God in her Precious Moments bedroom. "Thank you for Mommy and Daddy, and Grammy and Papa, all my brothers and sisters and my dolls, and all my cousins and aunties and uncles." Trina remembered she used to pray for her dog, Queenie, and her cat, Bailey. Her other grandmother and grandfather, and in later years her friends and boyfriends.

Chloe's room was a place of healing so that the pain of the first years of her life could be neutralized, and a new life built.

Still the tears came, and Trina allowed herself this one emotional breakdown. Sobs rocked her, and she cried silently, knowing now what Chloe was going through.

She'd gone mute because nobody had heard her. Everyone thought of her as a child, not taking into consideration how much she'd endured the first years of her life.

Reno and Dana had probably thought that they were rescuing the abandoned girl. But she had been traumatized by leaving her native home, moving away from all that was familiar, and then being apart from her sister.

Trina suspected the break-up of her parents' marriage, the absence of her mother's love, and the inability to get them to appreciate her need for stability had driven her to silence.

Trina thought of her happy home and the parents she relied upon even as an adult, and she knew Chloe couldn't go through that again. She would never turn her back on the child.

As the weight of her decision worked through her body, Trina remembered how good it felt to have Reno accept her apology. The joy she'd felt at Chloe's giggle.

The husky melody of her own voice as Reno had made love to her for the first time in eight years.

The creaks of his house as everyone slept but her.

The protest of her body when she'd gotten up to leave his bed.

She realized the lines of her life were connecting, and although her job was important, Reno and Chloe were now woven into her core.

She wouldn't leave.

With Chloe sound asleep, Trina tiptoed to the door. Quietly she let herself out, and looked one last time at the little girl who'd taught her how to love. Turning, she was engulfed by Reno.

He leaned into her, his hug so powerful it took her breath away. "Why won't she talk to me?" He pushed his face into her neck and chest. "I'm losing her." *To you.*

The unspoken words struck her hard.

"No," she whispered, emotional love welling again. "Never. She's coming back, Reno. She's healing. She's getting better."

Trina ran her hand over his back and arms. He had to know he couldn't be replaced. The pain that had been etched in his words shot from him in gulps of air.

Like a volcano, his pain flowed down her back, and she caressed him until he quieted.

"Come with me," she said softly.

Trina took his hand and she guided him back to his room. In the heavy silence she slipped off her coat and his clothes.

Naked, he guided her under the pile of covers, and he curled up behind her, covering them with the sheet.

Within minutes, his breathing evened.

The tip of a white plastic object stuck out from under the pillow. She tipped it up to see the baby monitor.

She looked over her shoulder at Reno, whose eyes were closed, and understood that she was taking on a lot of responsibility. She had a secure foundation. Her family had been deeply rooted in Georgia for four generations.

Now she wanted to help solidify the foundation of the Merriwether family.

Turning around, Trina put her arms around him and held on. He embraced her and she kissed him until he relaxed his grip. She soothed him as she had his daughter until he sighed.

"You're such a good father," she whispered, wanting to fill him audibly where silence had made him doubt.

She saw that his eyes were open. "You're a good father."

"I need you," he said.

Trina understood all that need meant. "Yes."

In a fluid motion, he sat up, bringing her onto him.

He put his hands on her bottom and urged her a little closer. He pulsed inside of her, and his exhale slid down to her breasts. His movements were measured and small, filling and fulfilling. Over and over he pulsed inside of her, bringing her closer. Their gazes locked as strong as a powerful embrace.

He kissed her above her heart, and her walls contracted, leaving her unprepared for the explosion that rocked her a microsecond before him.

Chapter 15

A glance at the calendar told Reno what he already knew. They only had two weeks before they had to be in Africa, and a week to get married.

He knew he shouldn't panic, but Trina didn't seem motivated to get the details of the wedding finalized. The ceremony was supposed to take place next Friday at her grandfather's office.

Reno eased his pen on the desk. He still didn't know the time, what to wear, or how far they were taking this wedding.

Were they inviting family to their sham nuptials, or was it a private ceremony?

His brain had been addled since the night Trina had agreed to be his wife.

The work on his desk beckoned him and he forced his mind back to work. The contract before him had put his business over the five-million-dollar mark in sales, and he wanted to celebrate.

He wanted to share his success with Trina, but he didn't know how to ask his fiancée to hang out with him.

He hadn't mentioned that he wanted her to be a real wife.

Frankly, he was afraid to push that envelope. She'd already turned him down once before; he was too close to being happy to deal with a setback.

The diamond ring in the safe made it official, so he just needed to see Trina.

After what he'd heard through the baby monitor the other night, he knew Chloe was getting better, but she still wasn't talking to anyone. And God knows he'd tried to bond with her.

Over the last two days he'd walked with her, talked to her, played with her, slept on her floor, hosted a tea party, and even had a sleepover with her stuffed animals in his bed, but she hadn't uttered a word. But she wasn't as sad, either.

He was grateful for that small change.

He'd initially planned that the other women would have very little contact with the girls after they returned from Africa. But Trina was different. She and Chloe had bonded in a way he hadn't. His daughter did things for Trina he'd pay money to have her do for him. Like laugh and pray and speak.

He couldn't very well keep Chloe and Trina apart, but putting them together would only be a set up for rejection in the future.

He and Trina needed to talk and set some ground rules.

Reno printed the contract he'd written for the other women and put it in his briefcase. He'd modify it and they could come to an agreement everyone could live with.

The phone rang and he picked it up. "Reno Merriwether."

"Sir, this is Mrs. Ayan Elmi."

"Good evening, Mrs. Elmi. What can I do for you?"

Reno braced his hand on the arm of his chair and sat up straight.

"Sir, we've had some unfortunate news."

"Is Christina all right?"

"Yes. The problem is that the orphanage is closing. It is in such a state of disrepair it has been condemned. All of the children have to be gone by Friday," she paused, possibly to steady her voice, "or they will be sent to other orphanages. After Friday we won't be able to guarantee she will be someplace where you can get her."

"Mrs. Elmi, I can't be there by Friday. The reservations have been made for weeks. I've already changed them once and other flights might be full."

"Sir, do what you can, please. She's been miserable the last few weeks and has been on the decline."

Reno leaned forward. "She isn't sick, is she?"

"She's sick, but not how you think. The doctor visited last week to give the children their shots, so she's fine, but she is sad. Please be here by Thursday, Friday morning at the latest. I have already put you on Friday's court calendar. The judge is making exceptions. I apologize, but I have other families to call, Mr. Merriwether. Shall we expect you?"

"Yes. Yes," he said, feeling real fear for the first

time in his life. Friday was April 30, the day Trina
was to find out the results of the SBO contest.

"When?" Mrs. Elmi asked.

"Thursday, for a Friday hearing. Please call me
if there's anything else."

"There won't be, Mr. Merriwether. I must go
now. Good-bye."

Anxious now, Reno paced, then headed back
to his desk and called the airlines. The flight was
packed on Thursday and first class was full. He
downgraded them to business class but four seats
together weren't available. Reno took three seats
and then the separate seat, hoping Mrs. Teralyn
didn't mind sitting alone. Might not be a bad
idea, he thought, adding them all to the first
class waiting list. He modified their reservations
for the return trip, including Christina.

Confirming everything one last time, Reno
wrapped things up when the doorbell rang.

Strolling down the hall, he noted that the sun
had begun to set, but that a nice breeze wafted
in from the patio. Maybe they'd eat outside.

He pulled the front door open. "Hey."

Seeing Trina again reminded him of why
dessert was so important. She was his chocolate
cake.

"I need a key," she said.

"Of course." Reno took the dresses from her
arms and set everything on the couch in the
living room.

"Is Chloe here?" Trina whispered, looking
down the hallway.

"No, she's at Mrs. Teralyn's granddaughter's
birthday party."

"Good. Mr. Dominguez, you can put these on the couch. Then let's put everything else in the master bedroom. Straight down this hall on the right."

"Excuse me, Mr. Dominguez," Reno said. "I need to have a word with Trina. Sir, can I get you a cold drink?"

"That would be nice." He laid the bags carefully on the couch.

"I'm sorry." Trina went over and took his hand. "It's almost time for your diabetes shot, but you have to eat first," she said in Spanish.

"I will be fine." Mr. Dominguez looked like a proud father. "Point me to your kitchen. I will find something suitable to eat."

"No, let me do it," she said protectively. "Reno, Mr. Dominguez has worked with Daddy for years. He takes excellent care of us, and he volunteered to go shopping with me, and I'm taking terrible care of him."

"You're a good girl. I won't starve."

"Shopping? My hat's off to you," Reno said.

Mr. Dominguez sat down heavily and Reno could see that he was about seventy.

"I love shopping with women. They want to know my opinion about their dresses and their shoes. I don't know so much about the stock market, but I know everything about beautiful women. You want to know? You ask me."

"We should have a weekly meeting," Reno said, and both men laughed.

Reno made the unsweetened tea they kept on hand for Mrs. Teralyn's husband, who was also a diabetic.

Trina served up leftover turkey and dressing, potato salad, tea, and warm rolls.

Trina turned on the kitchen TV. Reno liked how she moved, making sure he had everything. Mr. Dominguez sat down, watching TV, eating his dinner.

"Ready?" she said to Reno.

"Definitely."

As soon as they were behind closed doors, he couldn't keep his hands off her. He kissed her until he felt her body relax.

"Reno," she breathed against his lips, her hands caressing his head. "We have a problem."

His forehead touched hers and they shared a breath.

"You're right. We do."

"Let me go first," she said. "We received notice that the banquet to announce the winners for the SBO Contest is this Friday and not next. Somehow they sent out the date from last year's program. That's a huge problem because our wedding is next Friday. Speaking of, we have to decide if we're inviting people. We haven't talked about any of this, so I'm glad Chloe isn't here so we can get things straight."

Reno told himself not to panic. "We have a bigger problem."

The buttermilk colored suit looked enticing on Trina.

She draped her jacket over the chair back and sat down.

"How could there be anything worse than our fake wedding having to be moved?"

He chuckled at the irony. Taking her hands, he focused on her eyes.

"We have to leave for Somalia this Thursday. The adoption is this Friday. I just got the call. We have to get married tomorrow."

Trina stared at him. "It takes two days to get to Somalia. The best we can do is a hearing on Saturday. Do they understand that?"

"I didn't ask her. I reacted. All she said was the orphanage has been condemned. If she's not adopted by Friday, she'll be put in another orphanage, and Mrs. Elmi said I'll have a hard time finding her, let alone being able to adopt her. They're making an exception to have court dates this Friday."

"I knew we were cutting it close, but we can't possibly make it. There are no direct flights to Somalia. I checked. The best we can do is go into Kenya through Germany or land in Cairo and then to Somalia. Aren't there any other alternatives?" Trina paced, her hand on her hip, chewing her lip.

"I'm afraid not. They're not giving us any other choice. I believe if we tell them we will be en route, they will make an exception, but a whole day or a few days, I just don't think so."

"The awards," she said, sounding sad. She wouldn't make eye contact and stopped at the window Chloe looked out from so often.

This was what he'd been expecting. He'd thought all along that she'd renege and go for her own goals. And why not? He'd told her one date and everything had changed.

He'd thought they could work within their

careers and schedules to have a family, but he still might not get what he wanted.

He didn't want Trina to back out, but he saw she was embroiled in a private war.

"Trina, you agreed."

She fumbled in her purse. "I know, but we were on one timetable and now that's changed." She was completely distracted. "I know I promised, but I have a lot of things to do. This isn't just about me. My father was going hunting tomorrow. I need to catch him."

Reno had no idea where her thought process was taking her. "Why?"

"He's hunting with my grandfather. If Papa and Daddy aren't here, I can't get married tomorrow. No judge, no marriage."

Reno was ashamed of his thoughts. He'd been thinking only of himself. He didn't have an extended family to consider.

Trina hurried around Reno's desk and typed on the keyboard; then she tilted the monitor back.

"Can you log me on? I need to e-mail my family and let them know the wedding isn't next week, but tomorrow. Daddy?" she said into the phone. "Am I glad I caught you. Papa with you?"

"Yeah, girl. What's up?"

"Remember that situation I told you about with Reno and his daughters? Well, the timetable has been moved up. Think you and Papa can hold off going hunting until the day after tomorrow?"

"For you, yes. Now what do we need to do?"

"Have a wedding at Papa's house tomorrow?"

Trina held the phone up for Reno, who'd come to his desk to log her on to the computer.

"Baby girl, you'd better call your grandma and your mother for that."

"Okay, Daddy. I'll see you tomorrow."

Trina hung up and stared at the computer screen. "My father and grandfather will be there." She dialed her grandmother and started explaining everything. Her mother was there, so the explanation continued until questions were answered and the details set.

Sitting in his chair, Reno pushed back from the desk and Trina sat down on his lap. "Ooo."

He held her down. "Stay where you are. I'm comfortable."

"You're distracting me. Now stop," she whispered.

She started tapping on the keyboard and he watched her back move as she worked. Her hair was growing past her shoulders.

Reno tugged on it.

She typed, then stopped. "I don't know what to say. What are we doing, Reno? How do I explain this to my family?"

"Maybe you'd better—"

"Right." She got up and pulled the visitors' chair to the side of his desk.

"I'd have gotten that for you."

"It's no problem."

Reno reached inside the desk drawer and pulled out a jewelry box. A two-carat Lucia, emerald cut engagement ring sat in the midst of black velvet.

"First things first." He opened the box.

Trina inhaled sharply. "This is gorgeous. You didn't have to. Reno, it's exquisite."

"You're doing me the greatest favor of all. The ring is yours to keep."

"No," she said, shaking her head as he slipped it on. "I can't keep this. Without love, what does it mean? Let's just see if there's a way we can both get what we need out of this."

Trina admired her hand for a moment. "I've got my calendar, so let's put together something that will make us all happy. When's the flight?"

"Thursday. I just changed the reservations. We need to call and give them your passport number," Reno said. "The tickets were initially first class but they didn't have four together, so I took four in business class and put us on the first class waiting list."

"If our wedding isn't real," she said softly, "why are we going through all this trouble?"

"It's as real as you want it to be."

A sad smile pulled her mouth down as she gazed at her ring. Trina squared her shoulders. "There's no need to have everyone take off from work. Wait," she said. "Do you think the judge will want to see pictures?" she asked.

"Of what?"

"The wedding."

The thought had never occurred to Reno. "I don't know. We didn't show any the last time."

She nodded. "No pictures of my wedding. Reno, I just can't—"

"Trina?"

She looked up at him. "Reno, I thought we had more time. Now I have to figure out how I'm going to get everything else done."

"We're going to have pictures."

She studied him. "We are?"

"Yes, and a cake and family, and food. Call all your family and tell them we're getting married at 7:00 tomorrow evening, if that's good for your mother and grandmother. I think it would be nice to call Nancy and see if she'd like to get her catering business off the ground for our wedding."

Trina gave him a slow smile. He went to her and wished Mr. Dominguez was somewhere else. He took her in his arms. "I'm sorry."

"Thank you."

He kissed her forehead. "You're thanking me? I owe everything I'm about to become to you."

He pulled back, looking at her hair, then her face, wishing she could be completely his forever. "Even if it's fake, it will be the best fake wedding you'll ever have."

She nodded and didn't speak for a minute. "I bought dresses for us. One for Chloe, June the bear, and me. There are several different colors and sizes for Mrs. Teralyn because I couldn't really tell if she's a six or an eight. The store is on standby for shoes, but that was for a next week wedding. I can return the extra dresses when we get back. We'll be ready."

"Did you get me a dress, too?" He smiled from ear to ear.

"I'm not kidding," she said, running her hands up and down his backside.

"Why, Mrs. Merriwether. What are you doing?"

Trina slowly removed her hands and when she looked at him, her eyes were serious. "Don't call me that. I always imagined my Mrs. name in the real sense, and to know it's not real will just mess with my head. I'll go through the motions and make sure everyone is happy, but I can't keep hearing that, not from you. It's personal from you. Okay?"

"Okay."

Trina's honesty made him see how unselfish she was being.

"I'll call Nancy right now." Pushing her hair behind her ears, she picked up her BlackBerry. "Do you have an airplane ticket for me?"

"Yes. I've had it—"

"Go on," she said.

"For a while now."

"How long?"

"Since I met you at Intermezzo. I could have changed it, but I wanted . . . you. I'm going to make a couple of phone calls. I'll need a best man. I haven't got anybody. My friends were 'our' friends."

"People will surprise you. Why don't you give your old best friend a call? You never know." Trina held her phone to her ear. "Nancy, Trina Crawford. I hope you remember me because I have a catering job you might be interested in."

Trina gave him an affirmative thumbs up before stepping outside. Her ring sparkled, but there was no light in her eyes.

Chapter 16

"With this ring, I thee wed."

Trina said the words, but could hardly hear herself above the roar in her ears.

She wasn't going to pass out, but this seemed like a dream, and in a minute she'd wake up in her yellow bedroom, tucked into her comfortable king-size bed. Her grandfather wouldn't be standing on her left, her mother and father seated three feet away on her right.

She wouldn't be holding hands with Reno and Chloe, and Trisha, Tracey, and Shayla wouldn't be standing behind her in dresses they'd pulled from their closets at midnight last night.

More than anything she wouldn't be participating in a sham of a wedding, but instead she'd be working hard these last few days before the end of the SBO contest.

Trina opened her eyes and expected to see her room, but found herself standing in front of all of her smiling relatives. She looked at her grandfather and his eyes glowed with pride.

"By the power vested in me by the State of Georgia, I now pronounce you husband and wife. Reno Alexander Merriwether, you may kiss your bride, Trina Louise Merriwether."

Reno's lips touched hers.

Chloe stood in front of her new grandfather, between Trina and Reno, who held both her hands because she wouldn't sit with Trina's mother, and she wouldn't stop her tantrum with Mrs. Teralyn.

Trina looked down at the little girl dressed like a princess. For one year, she'd be her mother. She held her hands out and Chloe climbed up.

Trina kissed her. "I love you, Chloe Merriwether."

Love drifted from her to Chloe in a gentle wave and Trina could feel Reno's strong silent presence. He still said nothing. He still didn't want her the way she'd begun to want him. There was time, she thought.

"You're beautiful," he said.

She couldn't help how her heart raced every time she was this close to him. "Thank you."

The three stood before her family and a few of Reno's friends who'd come on short notice to support him.

"Excuse me, please," her grandfather said from behind them. Trina and her new family turned.

"May I introduce to you, Reno and Trina Merriwether, and their daughter, Chloe Merriwether."

Everyone applauded and the three walked down the divided aisle onto the patio where the sun was just beginning to set on the beautiful sunny day.

Trina still held Chloe on what should have been the happiest day of her life. She wanted to cry. Disappointment welled like the colorful balloons her little cousins blew up on the grass. "If I put you down, will you play with the kids?" she asked Chloe.

"She's never really played with anyone besides Mrs. Teralyn's grandchildren," Reno told her.

Trina's mother walked over and kissed her daughter on the cheek. Her eyes were glassy as she looked at her oldest daughter with her new granddaughter. Trina had to tell her what was going on, but her mother was the best secret keeper in the world. "Reno, Trina, you have my love and my babysitting time, except on Tuesdays and Thursdays because I have Tae-Kwon-Do classes."

"Thank you, Mrs. Crawford."

Keisha kissed Reno on the cheek. "My name is Keisha." She put her hand gently on Chloe's back and pulled a picture out of the elegant pocket from the silk suit she wore. She kissed Trina on the cheek. "Chloe," she said softly, "Trina is my baby. This is my daughter, and you are my first grandchild. Do you want to see a picture of Trina when she was a little girl no bigger than you?"

Chloe nodded. She tentatively looked at the photo, then at Trina and then at Trina's mother. "If you say Nana, that will be my name forever."

"She doesn't talk," Reno said.

"Yes, she does," Keisha said, not looking at her new son-in-law. "She'll talk when she's ready. Everybody knows that. Whenever you're ready," her mother said softly.

Chloe moved her lips and said, "Nana," but no sound came out.

Trina's heart leapt for joy. "Mama, did you see her? She tried to say, 'Nana!'"

"I certainly did. My grandbaby has named me." Keisha held her hands out for Chloe. "Will you give your Nana a big hug?"

"She—" Reno started but stopped when Keisha and Trina gently shushed him.

Chloe pulled her arms from around Trina's neck and went to her Nana.

Tears clouded Trina's eyes. "She doesn't go to anyone."

"I'm not anyone. I'm her Nana." Keisha hugged Chloe and rubbed her back while rocking her slowly. "Aren't you the sweetest girl in the world? My Trina was sweet like you. She had pretty eyes like yours, a pretty mouth like yours, pretty ears . . ." her mother said, while slowly moving away.

Trina's cousins guided Reno and Trina further onto the patio as they all watched the miracle in progress. Chloe didn't move, but listened to Keisha's voice as she learned to trust another person. The other aunts waited in line to love on the girl as they'd done for every child in the family.

"What will they do when there are two of them?" Trina wondered aloud.

Trisha and Tracey cleared their throats and gestured toward their matching dresses and they all laughed.

Chloe would be okay. Trina turned toward her cousins. "I need a tissue."

Reno pulled out his handkerchief. "Here,

Sweetheart." He dried her cheeks. "I can't believe she's letting someone else hold her. I kept her too sheltered this past year, but she had terrible tantrums if she thought I was leaving her. I got used to having her around."

Trina remembered his breakdown. "She's coming out of her sadness. They're all new, but she wants to know what's going on. She's always going to be yours, Reno. Look at her."

"She's not thinking about me."

"That's a good thing," Jake told him as he shook his head at the little boys who played on the lawn below.

"Did you have doubts that she'd ever come out of her shell?" Tracey asked Reno.

"This past year has been really hard. Chloe stopped talking when her mother left. She's only said one word and it wasn't to me. She hasn't spoken to me in a year and I miss her."

"She's on the way back, Reno. I know you can see that." Tracey watched Chloe and sighed. "Enjoy this. This family can work miracles on children."

"She said *home* to Trina and one night she giggled."

"Look at her," Jake interrupted. "She won't let anyone else hold her, but she'll let them touch her hand or her foot."

They all covered their mouths when their cousin Scooter, Shayla's little brother, came running into the room with a towel down the back of his collar. A big smile covered his face just before he launched himself off a chair.

His father caught him in midair, much to the surprise of everyone watching.

"Look at Chloe," Shayla said, laughing. "She's practically on top of Aunt Keisha's head trying to get away from Scooter. But she can't take her eyes off of him."

They all cracked up as the other women in their family tried to peel Chloe out of Keisha's hair. They cooed over her and she let them, pointing to her nose and ears and eyes.

"She knows her body parts," Reno said.

"She's letting others into her world. Just be careful that her reunion with her sister is slow and easy. She may not even recognize her."

Trina had always assumed that the girls would get along fine. "I wish you guys were coming with us."

"There's a lot we didn't think about," Reno said, taking Trina's hand.

Mrs. Teralyn came onto the deck. "Reno, Trina. I'm going home. Chloe is doing fine. She has grandmas and aunts and cousins. She is absolutely fine."

"Thank you for coming." Trina kissed her on the cheek. "Do you need a ride? I can have my cousin drive you home."

She shook her head. "No, dear. My husband is on the way. God bless you. I'll see you tomorrow at the airport."

Reno hugged Mrs. Teralyn tight, and Trina knew this was a big moment for him. She had so much family, and they were very much involved in her life. But Mrs. Teralyn was his only family besides Chloe and Christina.

Seeing Trina's grandmother in the doorway, Reno and Jake extended their hands to help her down the step. She curtsied, and Trina and her cousins giggled.

Grandma Vivian and Mrs. Teralyn walked down the deck stairs, chatting, as if they were old friends.

"They're adorable," Trina murmured.

"No one here is more beautiful than you," Reno said in her ear and kissed her.

"You keep telling me that, but I think you're biased."

His friends had come on the patio and Reno joined them, walking down the deck that stretched the length of the house.

The tuxedo made him look handsome and distinguished. If she hadn't already known the joy of making love to him, she would have been anxious, ready for the time when they could be alone. But she knew of the pleasure he could give her, and she knew if she wanted he would be hers any time.

But did she want him forever?

Her gut quaked and she felt hot. "Tracey, may I have something to drink?" Trisha and Shayla looked at her and Trina reached for them. "Nothing's wrong. I'm just a little warm."

Tracey handed her a glass of water. "What are we doing about the banquet Friday?"

"Do we have to talk about it now?"

"No," she said. "I just wondered if you wanted me to stand in for you? There's nothing that says you have to be present. And I think you getting married and adopting a child from Africa is a good reason to be absent. I'm just throwing it out there."

Shayla nodded as if giving encouragement to Tracey, whose voice had gotten softer, until she was whispering.

All three of her cousins looked at Trina. "Reno took me by surprise when he said we'd have to leave tomorrow. I wanted to win so badly, I couldn't see straight. But lately, I've had a change of heart about things," her cousins grinned at her.

"Certain family members have been honest with me about my being selfish and thinking I have to do everything by myself."

Trina reached for Tracey's hand. "You've been there from the very beginning. I couldn't think of a better person to attend as an equal partner in Suddenlysingle.atl. What do you think?"

Before Trina could finish her sentence Tracey was all over her in a tight hug. She'd known how much this would mean to Tracey, but it obviously meant more to the woman who'd begun to get help for her depression.

"I'm proud of you, Tracey. I love you."

Tracey stepped back, looking like her old self. "I'm honored. This is a great day, isn't it?"

"I'd like to ask a favor?"

Tracey looked at Shayla then Trina. "What is it?"

"If we win, will you call me?"

"I'll call you. The woman that's screaming at you, she'll be me."

"Well," Trina said. "It seems like I don't have anything to worry about. I can fly to Africa and everything here is taken care of."

"You sound sad," Trisha said, standing next to her sister.

"I'm not. I'm happy. It's just that I poured so much of myself into the company, it's hard to not be here for the finale. But with you all taking care of things, I know I don't have anything to worry about. There's Reno's friends. I'd better introduce myself."

Reno was talking to Jake, Eric, and Edwin, Trina's uncles who he'd just met.

Trina walked over and touched his arm. "Your friends are coming out."

Her uncles went down the deck stairs to settle down the younger children running across the yard.

He folded her hand under his arm. "Don't get too close. They're going to want to take you from me."

"You don't have anything to worry about."

Reno leaned over and pecked her cheek. "I can't wait to get you home."

"Later," she promised and extended her hand to his friend. "I'm Trina. Thank you for coming."

"Dwight Orr," the tall man said, reminding her of a young Colin Powell.

"George Osborne," the next man said.

"Honey," Reno said, "George owns seventeen car washes in Atlanta."

He called her honey, but she wondered when he'd really mean it.

"Clive Oliver," the last man said. "I'm a pilot for Delta. Which one of you ladies is single?" he said as he tugged on his pants a little. He was too lecherous for Trina's taste.

"Bride." Trina raised her hand and accepted another glass of punch from Tracey.

"Married," Shayla said, "And apparently just in the nick of time." Jake kissed his wife, laughing, as he lovingly massaged her hip.

Reno nudged Trina and she stepped to the side, wondering what Tracey was going to say.

"Single," Trisha said. "And, no thanks. I have to go boil my bunions. Excuse me." The family started laughing as did Reno's friends.

"You know you're wrong for that," Reno murmured as Trisha scooted by.

"Sue me," she said, and stopped at the top of the deck stairs. She smiled at the tall man, Dwight, and gestured with her head where she'd be. He nodded and quickly filled a plate of food before heading down the stairs. Trina looked over the railing and saw them head into the sunroom.

Tracey stood at the beautiful buffet selecting vegetables with care while Clive looked as if he wanted to make her a snack. When she was finished, she turned around with two plates in her hands.

"No, thank you," she said to Clive. "But if George would like to join me in the sunroom downstairs, I'd like that," she said softly. "I think I got enough for both of us."

The couple went down the stairs speaking in hushed voices.

"I can't believe the most beautiful women in the state just dissed me."

"You come on too strong. But you already know that and you don't want to change. One day someone will find that attractive, and you'll be happy. If you want you can join my dating company, Suddenlysingleatl.com, and we'll find just the right woman for you. I'm glad to meet you, Clive," Trina said, taking Reno's hand.

Clive studied Trina. "You're right. You can't be soft spoken in my business. I'm probably a little rough around the edges, but it works for me. I'll think about that dating site. Reno, thanks for the invite. Good to see you, man."

Reno shook his friend's hand. "You don't have to leave. It's still early."

"I have to fly to Singapore tomorrow. So I'd better get some shut eye. Trina, you're a good woman. I'll check you guys out after the honeymoon."

"Thank you. I hope I didn't hurt your feelings," Trina said.

"No way. One day I'll be as lucky as Reno." Clive jogged down the steps, over the yard to a car, and drove off.

"That was interesting." Trina turned to Jake, Shayla, and Reno.

"He looks like a good guy," Jake said. "Just too pushy for Crawford women. They like to do all the pushing."

Trina and Shayla pretended to go after Jake and backed him into the railing.

"I have a daughter to support," he reminded them.

"Only for Sienna." Trina and Shayla giggled, backing off. "You never told us what was burning in Mississippi."

Jake's face saddened. "The trailer we'd used

years ago as an office. A new group of doctors had planned to buy it and now it's gone."

"Sorry to hear that," Reno said. "Is there anything we can do?"

"Go get Chloe's sister. We'll take care of everything here. Where are you guys planning to live?" Jake asked.

Reno was reaching for her. She wondered if it was an unconscious movement and moved out of reach of his touch. Immediately, he turned and brought her to him.

"My house," he said, as did Trina.

"I'm keeping my house," Trina said.

"Why?" Jake asked at the conflicting answers.

"The same reason we live here and in Mississippi." Shayla was giving him her best shut up look.

"You're not selling your house? The market isn't that bad, is it?" Jake ate grape tomatoes, looking between them.

"Jake? I think we should go and check on Sienna," Shayla said.

"You can do what you want with your house." He finally looked at his wife. "Oh. I'll go check on my wife. Daughter." He corrected himself and walked into the house. "Why didn't you tell me to shut up?" he said as he passed Shayla.

They burst out laughing once he was inside. "He's adorable," Shayla said of her husband, "but so out of it. I'm going to nurse my baby and go home. I'm beat."

"Thank you, Shay," Trina said, hugging her. "I love you," she whispered.

"You're a gorgeous couple. I'm glad you found someone to love."

Trina pulled back from the embrace knowing Shayla was aware of the circumstances of their wedding. But Shayla embraced Reno, offering him sincere congratulations then went inside.

Lauren, Shayla's mother, who had been inside loving on Chloe went with her to the nursery to get Sienna. Perhaps Shayla was just going with the flow.

Trina looked around at the lantern lights, the elaborate display Nancy had set up on short notice. The family that had assembled on behalf of her wedding. The music.

She had to remind herself that they were fake, but for a good reason.

Trina stayed on the top deck with Reno, taking pictures as Reno promised, and greeting family members until dark.

Her mother volunteered to babysit Chloe, but they didn't want to push their luck. Taking both cars, they caravanned back to Reno's house, where Trina pulled up on the driveway unsure what to do besides drop off the gifts they'd return in a year.

Reno gathered Chloe in his arms, walked to the driver's door of her car and opened it. "Come in. This is our home now."

Trina got out, taking a bag of gifts with her.

She stood in the foyer, wearing her simple but elegant white wedding dress and didn't know what to do.

They'd never discussed the moment after the wedding.

June the bear was on the floor, and Trina walked to the door of Chloe's room. Reno stood over his daughter, tucking the covers. "I love you, Chloe Bear," he said to the little girl.

Trina touched his arm, wishing she hadn't. Memories of the last time assailed her.

"Thank you," Reno said, tucking June in, too.

Trina was halfway up the hall before he caught up to her.

"Come here. I want to show you something."

He guided her to a room off the hallway that she'd never seen before. He opened the door and they walked in.

The room was decorated in the same yellow color as her bedroom at her house.

"How did you know?"

"I asked your cousin your favorite color. After a serious interrogation where she actually pulled my credit report and criminal record, she finally gave me the colors of your room. I had this done because I want you to be comfortable here."

He traced her collar bone, down her shoulders to her hands.

"When did you have time for all of this?" Trina wanted to know. There were throw pillows and beautiful picture frames. "I know you're not super rich, so where's all this coming from?"

"Let me worry about that."

She looked into his eyes. "The wedding was gorgeous. Flowers, a photographer. Gifts for the girls and my parents. Reno, this is way—"

"Too much?" he asked, looking like Scooter, her little cousin.

Trina took his face between her hands. "No. Way more than I could have dreamed." She kissed him. "It's beautiful and thoughtful."

Reno brought her closer. "Of course if you want to share my—"

Reality dusted her like snowflakes in spring. "I would but—"

"You can't. I wish I didn't understand, but I do. Goodnight, Sweetheart."

"Goodnight."

With the door closed, tears poured from her heart for the only man she'd ever loved. And why she was letting him walk away, again.

Chapter 17

"Last call for Trina Crawford-Merriwether."

The loudspeaker blared Trina's name, but he didn't see her.

Reno fought the sickening feeling in his stomach.

"I'm sorry sir, but all the passengers have boarded. She's not here."

Having sent Mrs. Teralyn and Chloe ahead to be seated, Reno waited for Trina.

"Sir, you're going to have to board now."

"She's coming." He paced the gate area for a glimpse of his wife. Her cell phone went straight to voice mail for the thirteenth time. "Maybe she's stuck in security."

The agents didn't say anything. They'd probably seen this a thousand times.

Ms. Roberts came around the desk. "If she shows up, we'll get her on the first flight tomorrow."

"That's going to be too late. It takes about two days to get to Somalia. She's here. I can feel it. Maybe she got the gates confused."

Reno stood there, dodging the slap of defeat that chased him. The last three days had been too perfect. Last night especially, making love to his wife and having her sleep in his arms with no pretense and her not sneaking out.

All of his dreams had come true—except this one.

Trina had left early this morning, claiming she'd forgotten her passport at home. But she hadn't gotten back before they'd left for the airport. He'd left the house on her promise that she'd meet him here and had been growing more anxious since the last time he'd heard her voice.

"I can't leave without her," he said to Ms. Roberts, wondering how he'd deplane Chloe and Mrs. Teralyn. They were strapped in, and Chloe seemed happy. She hadn't fussed all day. Her eyes had shined with expectation as she glanced around every corner when she'd gotten up this morning. And when she'd seen her new aunt Trisha loading their bags into the car, she'd smiled at her and pointed to her new white sneakers.

Trisha had blown her a kiss and let it go into the wind. The Crawfords were an amazing family.

"Mr. Merriwether? Is the reason you're going to Somalia still there?"

"Yes, I'm adopting a child. A little girl."

"Then you have every reason to board. Don't let anything or anyone stop you from getting your family."

Reno remembered their lovemaking last night, the tender way Trina tucked Chloe into bed, and that she'd come to his room, not the one he had decorated for her.

Trina was there and he wasn't leaving without her. He started down the concourse ignoring the protests of the attendants.

Reno didn't care. He wasn't leaving without Trina.

Trina watched another plane take off and kept the disappointment to herself.

"What time is your flight?"

"It already took off. So this kidnapping thing was unnecessary, Drake."

She sat in the airport parking lot, her car blocked in by Drake's. He'd obviously followed her from her house to the airport.

Before today, Trina had never been afraid of him, but she'd underestimated him yet again.

When she'd seen him she'd hurriedly gotten back into her car, forgetting that he had a set of keys.

He'd let himself in and they'd been locked in her BMW for the past two hours. She tried not to think about Reno, who was probably worried that she'd changed her mind, or Chloe, whom she watched fall asleep last night. Or that her plane had probably left five minutes ago.

"Trina, you were always discounting my feelings," Drake whined. "This discussion was necessary because you owe me an explanation. How could you marry him and not me? Do you love him?" He laughed. "That's so funny. You can't. You dated me for over two years."

Trina wasn't sure how to answer that question. If she said yes she loved Reno, she wasn't sure if he'd lose his mind or walk away. She needed to be in one piece to get her new daughter.

"I love him," she said, being honest. "I love him. Now I have to go."

"What's so great about him? He has a kid and you don't want children." He laughed again, as if it were a no-brainer. "What does Mr. Bodyguard have that I don't?"

Everything.

"We could have had it all."

"I didn't want it all, Drake. It just didn't work out."

"You can't go. You have to stay here with me and give us the proper chance. Your family will understand an annulment."

"Drake, I'm leaving."

He grabbed her sleeve. "We're not done talking about this."

With her left hand under her leg, she pressed the speed dial to her father's phone again, praying that he'd called for help. In the last thirty minutes, no one had walked anywhere near her car. Not behind or in front.

She really hoped that meant that help was a step away.

"Get off my clothes, Drake or I'll hurt you."

"What, because you have a black belt? You can't beat me up, Trina. You're too civilized for that."

Beyond angry, Trina unbuckled her seatbelt and leaned back for her coat. Drake struggled with her and stopped, having successfully unlocked the doors to the car.

"Drake, I'm warning you."

"No! I'm warning you. I'm the head of this relationship and the sooner you recognize that the better. You don't love him. Say it!"

She suddenly saw Captain Jesse Alred, her father's friend of twenty years, in the side rearview mirror.

"I love him."

"*We* were in love," he whined, and she actually felt sorry for him.

"It wasn't the same."

"It could have been had you given us a chance. It's not too late, Trina. I'll try harder."

"Drake, it's over."

Captain Alred gave her the five finger countdown.

"It doesn't have to be."

"I love Reno. I'm not going to change my mind."

Trina barely got the last word out before her door was wrenched open, and she was dragged from her car.

Trina was escorted through the airport and to the gate. She pushed her hair from her neck, glad that her father was holding her hand. "Dad, how'd you get them to hold the plane for me?"

"Honey, a kidnapping doesn't happen every day. You're going to get there with no clothes, but don't worry, Mom and I will bring them in two days."

Trina stopped short. "You're coming?"

"We wouldn't miss meeting our granddaughter for any reason in the world. You've brought a special gift to the family, Trina. This is a big deal for all of us."

Tears slipped down her cheeks and she hugged her father hard.

"I love you all so much. Thank you."

"Mrs. Merriwether, we're glad to meet you," the flight attendant said, after having a discussion with several of her supervisors. "Ma'am, it's time to board."

"Okay." She hugged her father hard and shook the hands of the Atlanta police officers who'd escorted her to the gate.

She took her carry on and hurried onto the plane.

Trina could hear a child crying as soon as she boarded. Thank God Chloe was out of that phase. This was going to be a long flight, and the last thing she wanted was to hear a child crying the whole way.

She got to her seat and could see that Mrs. Teralyn was stressed out. Chloe was screaming at the top of her lungs.

She reached for Trina and she captured the squalling girl in her arms. "Hey, little angel. What's wrong?"

She sat down and rocked Chloe who still cried but was settling down. Trina could see she'd been crying for a while.

"Mrs. Teralyn, why is she crying? Where's Reno?"

She pushed her brown curls off her forehead, speaking in Spanish so Chloe couldn't understand. "Honey, he got off. Looking for you."

The plane rolled backwards, and as Chloe began to cry again, Trina cried, too.

Chapter 18

Trina loved Africa from the moment the plane touched down. She walked through the airport, an inner peace eclipsing her discomfort.

They'd settled into the hotel an hour ago and had called Mrs. Elmi, who came to the hotel to meet them.

"Where is Mr. Merriwether? Judge Lola Danage will only meet with you as a couple."

Mrs. Elmi stood inside the hotel lobby, having greeted Trina, Mrs. Teralyn, and Chloe, who looked out from behind Trina's legs.

"Mr. Merriwether was detained, but his flight is scheduled to arrive this afternoon," Trina lied. She'd been trying to reach Reno for hours. Her cell phone was supposed to have international coverage, but there was a problem, so she bought two at the airport and had left messages on her father's cell phone. She prayed he listened to his messages and would call her back.

Stress lines marked Mrs. Elmi's face. "He has to be here. He is scheduled for court at two today. An hour from now."

"Mrs. Elmi, I'm here, and I'm his wife. Is there a problem with the judge not being able to meet with us together, tomorrow? I know it's on a Saturday, but these are extenuating circumstances. We're flying commercial flights and we have to fly when they have space. I'd love to meet with her Honor today, and offer the judge and her staff dinner, and then we can finalize everything tomorrow once Reno gets here. Most of all, we'd like to see Christina."

"That is most unprecedented. I do not know if the judge is available and she does not accept any attempt to bribe her or the court. No. I will not take this to her."

Trina put her hands together. "Please don't misunderstand, Mrs. Elmi. I am not trying to bribe the court. I'm just asking for mercy as we were working with a very tight travel schedule that went awry. I understand the urgency with which we have to act, but I'm here, and Reno is on the way. We beg for an exception based upon some unfortunate circumstances. Please have dinner with us. My daughter is going to be hungry, and she will want to see her sister. Please, ma'am." Trina controlled the desperation in her voice. "Please don't keep the girls apart any longer."

Mrs. Elmi seemed to consider the impassioned plea. "How far away is he?"

"I believe Cairo." Trina asked for forgiveness for the lie. Nobody was anywhere to be found. The only person who seemed to know anything was Tracey, and she'd just said they were en route and the call was disconnected.

Last night as they'd flown, Trina had prayed,

and when she finished talking to God, it had been morning.

Chloe was on edge, the tiniest thing sending her into tears. The days of her being a silent crier were gone.

"Mrs. Elmi? When can I see my daughter?"

"I'm expected to make the introductions to the entire family." She worried her lip with her teeth.

"Most of us are here. We've come all this way. I promise Reno will be here."

Trina could only take the position that she was going to get what she wanted because if she didn't, her world would fall apart.

The older woman looked at Chloe. "Would you like to see your sister?" Chloe shrugged, and Trina and Mrs. Teralyn grasped hands. "Well, since you did come from America . . . Come. I will take you to her. But remember, nothing is final until mandated by the judge."

Chapter 19

The four women and the driver bounced around in an old Toyota that landed in every hole in the road. The country was war-torn and looked it. There were children in the streets, some of whom were almost bare, whereas others were in school uniforms. Poverty was a way of life. Even the animals looked sick with their ribcages as prominent as the children's.

Trina didn't miss a single thing. She rubbed Chloe's knee, and kissed June every time Chloe held up the bear. She wanted Chloe to be as comfortable as possible. Trina had no idea how she'd react to being back in her old home or seeing her sister for the first time in more than a year.

After bouncing around in the back of the car for an hour, they arrived at a wire gate. The driver, Larry, hopped out and opened the wire fence that seemed it could bar nothing.

"Are we here?" Mrs. Teralyn asked Mrs. Elmi.

"Yes. This is it."

"Where are the buildings?" Incredulity heightened her voice.

Larry got back in, drove a few feet, then got back out and closed the gate. It hardly seemed necessary, as four feet to the right the gate lay flat in the dirt.

"You will see," Mrs. Elmi answered, then spoke to Larry in a language Trina didn't understand.

Larry slowed. Two buildings were ahead of them and one was on the right, the first one made of a gray slab, broken in the front as if lightning had struck it.

"Was there a terrible storm?" Trina asked, watching in horror as children filed out of the building.

"War did this. That is the school and dorms for the primary age. The other building is for children under five. We put them all together because they are uninhabitable."

Trina looked at the building to her right and shook her head. One whole wall was missing, the door hung in a listless droop. Half the roof appeared to be gone.

A lady led children outside, and they looked on curiously.

Trina got the impression if she waved her arms they'd all come running. She was glad she was at least going to be able to save one.

"Stay. I will come for you," Larry told them over his shoulder.

Mrs. Elmi hopped out, and the driver cut off the engine. Trina hoped he wouldn't have the same trouble getting it started again that he did at the hotel.

"Sir, have there been many adoptions?"

"Five."

There were at least twenty children walking through the dirt.

"Will they be adopted?"

"Nobody has come yet."

"What is the language of the children," Mrs. Teralyn asked.

"It is called Common Somali. Many understand some English."

If the air wasn't so acrid, Trina would have exhaled a silent scream at the devastation these children lived in.

How could this be? She swallowed the lump and let Mrs. Teralyn grasp her hand in prayer. Trina passed her a twenty-dollar bill and gestured for her to give it to Larry. Mrs. Teralyn nodded.

Mrs. Elmi came out of the building and walked back to the car. Larry got out, opened the back door, and held out his hand for Trina.

"Mrs. Merriwether? Ma'am," Mrs. Elmi said to Mrs. Teralyn. "You will please follow me. We will have a meeting in here."

Trina thanked the driver and picked up Chloe who clung to her, but looked at the children with interest. Whenever they spoke, she turned her head and watched them.

Mrs. Teralyn pulled a large suitcase on wheels along with her. She stopped and talked to Larry, opened the suitcase, and handed him four plastic bags.

He thanked her profusely and got into his car. He drove off, then turned around in a big cloud of dust.

Trina and Mrs. Teralyn stopped and waited as

he ran very fast toward them. He thanked Mrs.
Teralyn again, and they said a few words. She
went back into her suitcase and gave him four
more bags. He bowed this time, tears in his eyes.

"He has eight children," she told Trina.

Trina nodded and they walked inside.

"What do you have?" Mrs. Elmi asked, curious.

"Goody bags," Mrs. Teralyn said, giving Trina
an excited glance. "We give them to children
when they visit our homes. Since we are visiting
the children here at their home, I thought I
would give them the same gifts. Is that okay?"

Mrs. Elmi nodded. "What kind of goodies?"

"Oh, well. Let's sit down and I will show you."

Trina couldn't have been more grateful for
Mrs. Teralyn. She'd thought of everything. Trina
had brought things as well, but everything was in
her bag.

Her parents would bring everything in a
couple days. She just hoped it was in time.

Mrs. Elmi showed them to a room with a desk
and two metal chairs.

Trina wanted to sit down because Chloe was
getting heavy from holding her, but the child
had been so quiet that Trina hated to disturb her
peace.

"Please, sit," Mrs. Elmi offered.

"You two go ahead. I think Chloe and I will
play over here." Trina lowered her daughter to
the floor and stretched her back.

Chloe watched and did the same. Trina
twisted her shoulders and sighed and Chloe
copied again.

"You silly goose." Trina poked her. "You've been quiet all day."

Chloe shrugged and waved her hands in the air.

Mrs. Elmi burst out laughing and Trina turned.

Mrs. Teralyn was blowing bubbles from a little bottle and wand in her hand. The older woman laughed gleefully and the tension left Trina's body.

She heard footsteps and Chloe moved behind Trina's pants-covered legs.

"Good afternoon. I am Mrs. Bakrin, and I am the principal here."

Trina and Mrs. Teralyn shook hands with the proud-looking woman.

"Thank you for your kind welcome," Trina said. "I'm Mrs. Trina Merriwether, and this is my daughter Chloe and our family friend, Mrs. Teralyn. Due to an unfortunate circumstance, my husband, Reno, was delayed, but he's on his way to join us here so that we can meet our new daughter."

"What unfortunate circumstance?"

"Pardon?" Trina asked.

"We expected him today. Is all well?"

"Yes, ma'am. I was delayed getting to the airport and my husband went to look for me in the airport. I caught the flight, but he missed it." Trina tried to smile. "He's on his way."

"You were late?"

"I was. Mrs. Bakrin, I was involved with a man who couldn't accept the word *no*. He kept me against my will in the parking lot of the airport. My husband went to look for me and once my situation ended and I got to the gate, Reno was nowhere to be found."

"That is unfortunate. I'm glad you're all right. What time will he arrive? Your court time is two o'clock."

"He'll arrive tomorrow."

"Oh no," Mrs. Bakrin said. "That is much too late. We are closing today."

Panic hit Trina's body like shrapnel. "I understand the circumstances, and would love to take everyone to dinner and explain myself to the judge. We respect the rules, but beg for mercy, Mrs. Bakrin. It's not Reno's fault. Please don't penalize him for my . . . problem. He's been waiting for this day for so long. I can't bear to break his heart. Please." Trina waited, ready to meet any demand for another chance.

"It is not my decision to make. The judge will decide and I am not sure she will want to speak with you outside of the courtroom."

"If you would ring the judge's clerk, I'll be glad to let her speak to my grandfather in Atlanta, GA. He's a judge, too, and he married Reno and I. He can assure her that my intentions are pure, and that my husband and I so badly want this little girl to join our family. Here is his number, and my phone card number. Please give him a call and explain where you're calling from. They will put her right through. If you all can't do dinner, I would love to invite you for coffee and dessert."

Mrs. Bakrin smiled. "It is not money that you can throw at us, Madam. It is too late for that."

"You're so right, Mrs. Bakrin, I apologize if I offended you, but we have to eat, so I was inviting you. We also brought goodies for all the children. These were leftovers from a party for my nephew and little cousins and were just sitting at my mother's house. Do you think the kids will enjoy playing with bubbles?"

"I-I don't know." The well-attended woman looked on curiously. "Let me see."

Mrs. Teralyn blew a few into the air and the two women started laughing.

"They will love this. You have more to share?"

Trina nodded, keeping her hands folded and her excitement under control. "We have lots more. For all the children. Can you please ask the judge for my forgiveness and to please meet with us tomorrow?"

Mrs. Teralyn started unloading hundreds of bottles of bubbles, miniboxes of soap, baby wipes, toothbrushes, and toothpaste from her suitcase onto a desk. When the tester bottles of perfume fell out of the suitcase, along with minipads and hand lotion, Mrs. Bakrin walked over to the desk and fingered the items.

"I will call now. Just a minute. You will be available if she must speak with you?"

"I'm not leaving."

Trina finally sat down. Chloe climbed into her lap and showed Mrs. Bakrin her shoe.

"Very pretty," she said, and her breath caught. "She is from—"

"Yes, ma'am. She's from this orphanage."

She put her hand to her mouth and stared. "I will return momentarily."

The room was stifling hot, perspiration dripping down Trina's brow, but she stayed inside.

Even when Mrs. Elmi and Mrs. Teralyn went to give the children the goody bags.

From the cheers outside, the children enjoyed the treats, but Trina kept her anxiety under wraps. After all he'd done for her, and then he missed the plane because of her, she wasn't leaving without his child.

Forty-five minutes passed and Trina felt lightheaded. Chloe was getting antsy and wanted to get down, but a bug had sent her crawling back into Trina's lap.

"Honey, it's just a bug. He's more scared of you than you are of him."

Chloe wasn't buying it, and neither was Trina. There were bugs everywhere.

An hour passed and Trina stood up, her back hurting from sitting in the chair. She and Chloe walked to the door of the building and looked out. Many of the kids were being loaded into an old school bus, and were waving, smiling.

"Where are they going?" Trina asked, stepping outside for only a second.

"To another orphanage," Mrs. Elmi said, looking after the children who called to her and waved. "That was a nice send off. Thank you, ladies."

"Where's Christina?" Trina's voice had edged into a panic and she handed Chloe to Mrs. Teralyn. "Was she on the bus? We have to get her back."

"Ma'am. Please calm yourself. She is here. Ten children remain, but they are sick and cannot go to the new orphanage. There are two other girls that I am taking with me. She is with them."

Three girls stood in the doorway of the

ramshackle former school, the smallest one in the middle.

She was skinny, but about the same height as Chloe. Her hair was shorter and she was a little darker. She didn't look up, but Trina knew who she was right away.

Mrs. Elmi called out and waved the girls over.

They got about five feet from Trina when she heard Mrs. Teralyn exclaim and begin to pray.

Trina covered her mouth as she knelt down.

She was looking at Chloe's twin.

Chloe, whose new home was behind Trina's legs, looked at her sister, walked over, and started speaking to her in Common Somali. Then she hugged her.

Chapter 20

Reno landed and went in search of his luggage, but found that a man had already been hired to get his bags. He stepped back and waited for his new in-laws to deplane from their chartered jet.

He could hardly believe the last twenty-nine hours.

Trina's father had explained everything and had given Reno enough reason not to leave the airport and go kick Drake's butt.

But his family was on their way to Africa, and he was, too.

When he'd missed the plane, he'd thought his life was over.

Getting a new reservation was impossible. He'd blown his opportunity and poor Mrs. Teralyn, on her way to Germany, the first stop on their trip, with a baby that wasn't hers.

Just imagining the story the older Hispanic woman would have to explain sent him into overdrive.

Then he saw Crawfords. At least ten of them at the gate, looking official and angry.

Trina's father had stepped up and explained what had happened, but that Trina had made the flight.

Reno hugged him. The impulse had shocked him. He'd been without a father for fifteen years, but Julian Crawford must have understood because he didn't let Reno go without reassuring him that Trina would handle everything once she landed.

Then the Crawford clan moved into action. They were escorted to a private meeting room at the airport. Reno sat in an executive chair around an oval table.

"Trina will handle the meeting with Mrs. Elmi. Reno, she briefed me on the way to the airport on your conversation last night."

Reno nodded. He hoped not. He'd talked very lovingly to his wife. Certainly not things she'd tell her father.

"She was expecting you to meet with Mrs. Elmi and then go to the orphanage, correct?"

"Yes, sir. The problem is with the judge. Our meeting was scheduled for tomorrow, and I won't be there. We were already asking for an exception to have it the next day, but I won't be able to get a flight."

More Crawfords and police officers came into the room.

Julian and Eric, Shayla's father, both pulled

out cell phones. "I'm waiting to hear from Nick," Julian said.

"I've got him," Eric cut in. "What's the status?" He listened and hung up. "Reno, I know this is a quick initiation into how the Crawfords can take something over, so I apologize in advance. You're still in charge, but we want to help."

The air was intense and quiet. All eyes were on him. "Go on. I'm listening."

"Nick has a friend who has a private jet. It seats twenty. He's willing to loan us his jet to take you to Africa."

"What?"

"Nick has a friend—" Eric started again.

Reno waved his hands. "No, I got that. A friend has a jet." He laughed and rubbed his forehead. "I have friends who have racquetballs and don't lend them out."

"We know this is a lot to swallow at one time. If you want us to back off, we'll walk away right now. This is your situation," Julian said.

Reno rubbed his upper lip. "What else?"

"We would like to go with you," Eric said. "Jake and I are a part of Physicians Without Borders, and one of the places I've always wanted to go to is Somalia. We've worked in other parts of Africa, but not Somalia. When the adoption happens, your daughter will have to be held for about ten days. We'd like to come out, help the children and see if there are others that need help. Of course, it's up to you."

Reno was speechless. He wasn't a man prone

to crying, but he felt like he'd been given his life back. "Of course I accept your offer and you can come. All of you. When do we leave?"

Julian looked at his phone. "I believe my wife and mother have just arrived at the airport. Is right now too soon?"

"Right now is great."

Chapter 21

Reno boarded the plane and tried not to look shocked. The jet was more luxurious than he ever imagined. He'd always thought first class was the top of the line, but now he knew there was a life he'd never known existed.

There were captain chairs, comfortable couches, a bedroom, and a full bathroom.

Late last night while they flew over the Indian Ocean, Jake had sat beside him and explained the facts of life—after marrying a Crawford.

"You know this is just a part of life, right?"

Reno looked at him. "A life I used to dream I'd one day have."

"And now you do, but don't get uptight about it."

"I'm not," Reno said, but his shoulders were tense, his back hurt even though he was in the most luxurious chair he'd ever sat in.

He needed some Tylenol for his headache. "Okay," he lowered his voice. "How can I not? I can't give this to her. This is exactly why I stopped dating her in college."

"I didn't know you and Trina had that kind of history."

Reno nodded and accepted white wine from the flight attendant.

"We dated her freshman year, my sophomore. She wanted me to stay at UGA, but I wanted to go to Michigan. I left her."

"And today, you thought she'd left you."

"Yep. I'm an idiot, Jake. I left her twenty voice mails. Who knows if she's going to want me after she hears them."

"You didn't tell her to get lost," Jake said, his expression braced for the worst.

"No. I said just the opposite. I was sorry for painting her into a corner. I didn't mean to make her miss her big evening just to help me. I was selfish. I loved her. It got pretty sloppy. I was pathetic."

Jake laughed and so did Eric who was passing by and overheard their conversation. He gave Reno's shoulder a squeeze and kept going.

"Jake, are these brothers for real?"

Jake nodded without looking at them. "Yeah, we are."

Reno leaned his chair back and relaxed. "I guess I should just enjoy the ride."

Jake nodded. "Now you got the picture."

Trina sat on the desk of the administration building watching her girls get to know one another.

Developmentally, Christina was behind Chloe, who chattered nonstop in a language Trina couldn't understand. She held her sister's hand and made Christina hold June, and every time she dropped the bear, Chloe would chatter away, while retrieving the bear and putting it back under Christina's arm.

She showed her sister how to drink out of a sippy cup and she touched her sister's hair.

Christina smiled here and there, then laughed when she tried to show Chloe a bug, and she screamed her head off.

She body crawled up Trina, who was dirty from being walked on, sat on, and touched by four hands and feet.

Mrs. Bakrin had come back hours ago saying the judge spoke to her grandfather and had granted the new hearing, but she declined dinner. She didn't want it to seem like favoritism.

She also declined Trina's request to take Christina back to the hotel. So Trina had sent Mrs. Teralyn and Mrs. Elmi back to eat and rest at the hotel. The two women had bonded. They were both hardworking women who would do anything for their countries and their families.

Trina was proud to know them.

Mrs. Bakrin had stayed behind one more night to see that the sick children would be picked up and taken to a local area. She said there wasn't much hope for them, and Trina couldn't bring herself to examine them yet, but after her girls went to sleep, she'd go over and check on them.

She checked her cell phone and was surprised to get a signal. There were twenty-seven messages.

She thought of answering voice mail to get a fix on Reno's location, but decided to call her mother instead.

Trisha answered. "Hey! How are you?"

"Chloe has a twin, Trisha. She's a twin."

"Oh my goodness. How'd they get separated?"

"I don't know," Trina said, watching the girls walk with their arms around each other's waists. "They are so cute."

"That's great, but I have even more good news for you," Trisha said excitedly. "You won the contest!"

"We won?" Trina covered her mouth, thrilled with the news. "I can't wait to see you and Tracey so we can celebrate."

"I know," Trisha said.

"Trisha? Trisha?"

Trina looked at the phone and sighed. The signal was fading. "Do you know where Reno is?"

"On the—"

The beeping sound pealed and the signal was gone. She closed the phone. "Come on girls. Time for bed."

Chloe came over talking away, but said nothing Trina could understand. "Honey, Mama doesn't know that language."

"Mama," Chloe said.

Christina looked up at her. "Mama?"

Chloe shrugged and started speaking gibberish again. Trina bent down and listened. It wasn't gibberish. It was Common Somali. "Yes," she said to Christina. "Mama."

She held her hands out and Chloe held her fingers. Christina didn't and Chloe walked over

and put her sister's hand in Trina's. Then she
came back and held Trina's other hand.

The girls were fast asleep under stars that
looked like the ones from home. The same ones
on which she'd wished for cars and jewelry and
things. Trina knew she was a world away, but
while she was here she needed to help.

She closed the door so animals wouldn't get
into the dorm room where her girls slept and
walked over to the other building that acted as a
school, with a curtain dividing the learning area
from the infirmary.

The children in there were awake, some with
their eyes open and somewhat alert, whereas
others looked a step from death. The stench was
palpable, but she ignored it. She didn't feel or
smell spring fresh either.

She left and returned with their bags. Trina
pulled out baby aspirin and bottles of water,
bandages, and wound dressings. Several of the
little ones had temperatures; others were so dehy-
drated, she knew a bottle of water wouldn't be
enough. She decided to put her nurses training
to good use and help while she could.

She'd left Emory nursing school with one class
left to finish years ago. She'd lost interest almost
as soon as she'd entered the program, but she
hadn't wanted to let her family down.

Before she started working on her dotcom, she
finished that last class and had sat for her
boards. Her family didn't know, and she'd never
tell because she had no desire to pursue nursing

in any capacity. But tonight she called upon the education she'd gotten and helped the children.

Two of the girls were covered in infected bites and Trina cleaned and dressed their wounds and filled them with water and a dose of acetaminophen. She broke crackers into bite-size pieces and fed them while whispering soothing words.

When each was fed and cleaned, Trina blew bubbles and talked to them. Afterwards, she cleaned her hands and went outside where she cried until her well was dry.

Then she text-messaged her whole family repeatedly, hoping someone would get the message. *Kids sick. Send Jake, Eric with meds, bandages, water. Please.* She hit send ten times, hoping against hope someone would get the message.

Going back into the dorm with her girls, Trina lay on the cot and waited for the cavalry to come.

Chapter 22

"Mrs. Teralyn, where's Trina?"

Reno looked at his nanny who was dressed and ready to go, but nodding off in the lobby of the hotel.

Trina and Chloe were nowhere to be found.

"Oh, God is good. She is at the orphanage."

"I thought they were closing it down," he said, noticing Trina's suit in a bag.

"They did. They took the kids away, too. Except Christina. They wouldn't let us bring Christina with us, so Trina stayed behind."

"By herself?" he nearly shouted.

The rest of the Crawford men gathered around.

"Si," Mrs. Teralyn said. "She would not let me stay, Reno. She sent me back to rest my feet. I brought her clothes down here, and Chloe's so we can go get them."

She smiled and hugged each of the men. "You have brought the cavalry. She sent a message to my husband who called me in the room."

"What cavalry?" Reno asked, looking at her father and uncles and brother-in-law. "How does she have your husband's cell number?"

"I gave it to her, of course. I don't know how to answer those things so he calls me and tells me what they say."

Eric hung up from his conversation with Lauren. "Trina sent out a blast to bring supplies to help the kids. They're sick."

Reno looked down at his phone and saw that it was off. He'd forgotten to turn it on once he'd gotten off the plane.

"We need to get over there. Mrs. Teralyn? How far is it?"

"A half hour. But we have a ride. Well, not for everyone, but Larry will drive us."

The beaming young man came and introduced himself. Reno could see everyone's reaction to Larry's small car. But he got in with Mrs. Teralyn and Jake who carried a big medical bag.

"We'll meet you over there," he said to Julian and the rest of the family.

The ride was long and dusty. If potholes didn't swallow the car, there were hungry birds circling, contemplating their next meal. Reno couldn't wait to get out, but had to hold on another twenty minutes before the car stopped in front of a wire fence. As before Larry hopped out and opened the fence. Then he drove four feet inside the gate, stopped, and closed the gate.

Reno didn't complain. This was how things were done.

Jake talked to Larry in his native tongue and Reno looked at him. "I studied a little when you fell asleep. Larry, please take me to the sick children."

Reno got out and peeled off a few bills and gave them to Larry.

His bottom nearly hit the ground and Jake and Reno helped him up. Larry tried to return some of the cash, but Jake assured Larry that he was meant to have the money. The man turned off the engine, sat in his car, and cried.

"Trina?" Reno called. "Trina, where are you?"

Trina appeared in the door of a broken building. She ran to Reno and he embraced her.

He was whole now. His life had meaning. He wouldn't ever let her go.

"I'm sorry. I'm so sorry about Drake and making you miss your flight. I love you, Reno. I really do." she said repeatedly.

"I love you, too."

"I tried really hard."

His body went cold. "Where are the girls? Are they sick? Jake is here, honey. He can help them. Where are they?"

Trina wiped the tears from her eyes. "Our girls? Girls," she called.

Hand in hand, Chloe led her sister outside. She took one look at her father and ran straight at him. "Daddy!"

Reno scooped her up and squeezed her neck. "Say it again, Chloe."

She tried, but couldn't.

"Honey, you're squeezing her too tight."

"Hi, Daddy."

Reno buried his face in her neck. "Hi Chloe Bear."

"Daddy you're funny."

"Honey, this is Christina," Trina said softly.

He took one look at his other daughter and shook his head.

"Twins? Well, this is my lucky day. How do I have twin girls? I'm the luckiest man alive," he said, letting Chloe stand up.

She went to her sister and talked to her in Common Somali. He looked at Jake and Trina. "She hasn't forgotten."

"No, she hasn't. Trina, where are the sick children?"

"Inside here. I stabilized them and administered basic first aid. Everybody's stabilized, but I don't have any more supplies. They need a hospital. I don't believe anyone's coming for them. I think leaving them was the plan all along."

He looked in on the children. "Basic first aid? LPN?" he asked quietly.

"RN. Just passed. Don't tell anyone. I don't want to study medicine. I did it because mom's a nurse. Nobody knows that but a few of us. I finished my last class and sat for my boards so I could tell myself I finished something."

"It's your secret to tell, Trina. Now I think you'd better go see about your family and let me take care of these kids."

She hugged Jake. "Thank you."

* * *

The courtroom wasn't what Reno expected, but nothing had been. He thought it would be *Law & Order* style, but that TV myth wasn't how it looked in Somalia. The judge sat behind what could only be described as a lunchroom table with chairs facing her.

They sat with their counsel, while a court reporter recorded every word.

"You've only been married a few days."

"Yes," Trina said, "but, we went to college eight years ago. That's where our love began. It just took some time to figure out that we wanted each other."

"What makes you think you'll stay together?"

"No one can predict that," Trina said, speaking over Reno. "But my grandfather and grandma have been married about sixty years. My mother and father have been married about thirty years. They're here."

"Your parents?"

"Yes, ma'am."

Julian and Keisha waved at the judge and she smiled. "Why?"

"They have a new granddaughter, if your honor judges it to be so. My uncles and cousins are here. My brother-in-law is part of Doctors Without Borders, and he's tending to the sick children at the orphanage," she gestured for her family to wave.

"The point I was making was that I may not

have been in a marriage before, but I sure have good role models."

"And you, sir," she asked Reno. "Your wife is quite an advocate of marriage. Two girls, Mr. Merriwether? How are you going to handle that?"

"I love them as if they were mine from their first breath. I've worked hard to get the family together and with the help of other family, we're here, ready to make Christina ours forever."

She reviewed the files and studied the family quietly.

"Does anyone have anything else to say?"

Chloe raised her hand. Reno and Trina chuckled and the judge turned her attention to the child. "Yes, young lady?"

She stood up on the chair and seemed to be showing off her pretty white dress with the pink bow at the waist.

"Trina, Chloe," she said pointing to herself. "Trina, Christina," she said, pointing to her sister.

She looked at her father. "Daddy," she said, then slipped back into a mix of languages Reno didn't understand.

"Hi, baby," Reno said.

"Please excuse my daughter. She went through a lot this past year and she just started speaking again."

"I know exactly what she said, sir. Do you?" the judge asked.

Reno had no idea. "Uh-no."

"Well, I do. This is the most unusual hearing

I've ever presided over. We have three generations present, and one a call away," she inclined her head toward Trina.

"But one I'm happy to see. It is my hope that this family grows and prospers. It is so ordered that your daughter's request will be granted. Her new name is Trina Chloe Merriwether, and her sister's name is Trina Christina Merriwether. You will now and forever be the daughters of Reno and Trina Merriwether. Mr. and Mrs. Merriwether, you may take your new family home."

Epilogue

The sun had begun to fade on the bright summer sky, but Chloe and Christina's energy hadn't. They splashed in their baby pool, giggling and playing a little girl's game of tag around the yard. Trina sat on her umbrella-covered lawn chair in her swimsuit, her feet in the baby pool, eyes shielded by sunglasses, a big floppy hat on her head, exactly where the girls wanted her.

Christina looked so happy. She was still smaller than Chloe, and still getting used to eating more than once a day. She ran to the snack table and picked up a grape, studied it for a moment before popping it into her mouth, then took off running again.

"Chew," Trina urged from her pool seat. "Chew."

Christina zipped by on quick legs, her cheek poked out with the grape. Trina got up and chased the little girl who giggled happily. Snagging her, she pulled her to her chest and kissed her cheek.

"No running with food in your mouth, Little Bug. Chew."

Christina giggled and finally chewed her grape.

"You're a sweet girl," Trina whispered in her ear, kissing her cheek. "Mama loves you."

When she'd first come home a year ago, Christina was apprehensive about getting kisses and hugs, but Chloe wasn't having it. She hugged her sister whether she wanted a hug or not. Christina had finally come around because Chloe wasn't going to have it any other way.

Chloe swung on Trina's legs. "Me, too. I want kisses too, Mama."

Trina lifted Chloe in her other arm and kissed her jaw. She rubbed her nose against her daughter's cheek. "I love you, Little Bug."

The girls' hearts beat quickly from exertion, but both were relaxed, content as they'd never been before.

Trina wiggle-walked them around the yard and their laughter bounced off the fence and lifted her heart. They ended their walk back at the baby pool where she sat down in her chair with them. Her life was so different than she had ever planned it to be. She was a mother of two little girls who adored her, and she couldn't imagine a day without them.

The sliding screen door opened and closed and she whispered to the girls. "Pretend to be asleep so we can scare Daddy."

All three went limp, their eyes closed.

"I don't see my angels," he said. "Trina-Chloe, Trina-Christina, where are you?" Trina started smiling as their little legs bounced with excitement.

They could hear him coming and a bag rustling. Their legs were moving faster and Trina knew they wouldn't hold out much longer. "One, two, three!" she said and they screamed, "Rah!"

Reno fell to his knees holding his chest. "I'm so afraid. You two scared me. I guess I'm going to have to eat my fruit bars by myself."

"No," the girls yelled in voices that chimed in equal timbre.

Trina looked at the man she loved with all her heart. "You're trying to bribe my girls and we're not falling for it, Daddy. Are we, girls?"

"Yes," they chimed.

Reno laughed.

"No," Trina urged, loving their game. "You can make it up to us by giving us all kisses."

He kissed each girl on the cheek and helped them down. They were in the bag of bars, tearing into them and walking off hand-in-hand.

"Now for you, Mrs. Merriwether. About that kiss . . ."

Trina met his lips with a tenderness that belied every encounter she had with Reno. He was the nicest, most loving man she'd ever known. "I love you, Reno Merriwether."

"Trina, baby." He kissed her neck, pulling her close. "Is it the girls' bed time, yet?" he asked hopefully.

She giggled as he nibbled her earlobe. "Not for another three hours, so cut it out," she murmured, stretching into him. "Shayla and Sienna are coming by, and so are my mother and grandmother."

Reno kissed her lips again. "I love your family, but Baby, can we postpone them for an hour. I need you," he groaned. "If I have to wait half the night to be with you, I don't think I'll make it."

She caressed his jaw. "Focus on the reward," she said, wrapping her arms around his neck. She held him close and ran her hand in lazy circles across his back. "You finished working?"

"Yes. The office is yours. Tracey sent a text message for you to call her at home."

Trina loved the setup she and Reno had worked out. Both companies were so well established, they worked in half-day shifts. Since the day was over, she needed to check e-mail and finish up some paperwork.

Suddenlysingleatl.com was a big success in large part because Trina had sold half the company to Tracey. She worked full-time and Trina part-time, until the girls went to school next fall.

"Are she and George stopping by?" Trina wondered.

"No. She said they were going out to dinner," he said, rubbing her warm leg. "You've been outside too long."

Trina kept her eye on the girls who sat on their canopy-covered swing together, talking. They still spoke a fair amount of Common Somali, but interspersed were English words.

"I'm out here as long as they are." She looked around the yard full of toys, the sand pit, the child-size lawn furniture her mother had insisted on buying, and she knew her life was blessed.

"You've been wonderful for Tracey. I'm just glad she's through that bout of depression."

"Me, too. She's a great lady. She just needed to come to grips with the mistakes she'd made and forgive herself."

"I never did find out what really happened."

Reno pursed his mouth. "I don't know every detail either, but whatever it was, she's better, and that's what counts."

The sun receded west and the outdoor lights on the patio flickered on. The girls chimed, "Barbecue, barbecue, barbecue," and Trina giggled when Reno frowned and smiled at the same time.

"I don't know who those mini-divas think they are."

"They are the loves of our lives and I think they want barbecue for dinner again."

"We've had it for a month straight."

"You know what the doctor said, 'let Christina eat when she feels like it.' Obviously she's hungry."

"Are my grandbabies outside?"

The girls hopped off their swing and ran for the screened porch door and their grandmother and great-grandma. The women scooped up the bouncing bundles of joy, kissing them. Sienna toddled through the door, looking at her cousins.

Reno moved to stand, but Trina captured his wrist and he brought her up with him. She could hear her father and grandfather talking to Shayla, Jake's voice calling out for Reno in the house.

"I love you, Reno Merriwether."

"God knows I love you, too."

The noise level increased as her family poured onto the patio, a mixture of laughter and love binding them.

Trina kissed Reno one more time, knowing life didn't get any better than this.

More of the Hottest
African-American Fiction from
Dafina Books